Beyaluna Burns

a collaborative novel

by Lindy Baker, Emily Fertic, and Gracie Sanchez

a project of the 2015-2016 Collaborative Novel Writing Class at Class Source of Tampa, instructed by Mrs. Crystal Crawford

Cover by Jason Crawford of Fierce, Inc
(http://wearefierce.net)

Contents

Dedications

Thank you to my mom and dad for letting me stay up past my bedtime to finish my writing homework, and kudos to my little brother for believing in this project (and me) from start to end and always offering his help. You three are the best, and when I get rich from the novels I write I'll buy you cool stuff (this includes pizza and cupcakes). I also want to thank our teacher, Crystal Crawford, for 1) having unfaltering faith that we could pull this off in less than one semester, and 2) guiding us inside and outside of our class time. Without her focus and dedication we'd still be daydreaming about writing a novel. (Don't worry, Crystal, I haven't forgotten to buy you pizza and cupcakes too.)

– Lindy

I want to give a special thank you to my friends and family that support me. Thank you, grandmother, for always being the most excited to read what I've written. Thank you, Negin, for always being willing to beta read and never sugar coating anything. Thank you, Lindy, for all of the endless brain storming sessions after class. An extra special thank you to the novel writing group, Lindy, Gracie, and Mrs.Crawford. Without all of us together, Beyaluna wouldn't exist and class definitely wouldn't have been as fun. "When our powers combine!"

– Emily

I would like to dedicate this to Lydia and Anastasia. Thanks for inspiring me to love writing and reading. Also, thanks to Audra and Katie for introducing me to *Hunger Games*. That book is still my favorite. I love ya'll.

– G.S.

Acknowledgements

The editor and writers of this book would like to thank those people who truly went above-and-beyond in support of our project.

To Mrs. Dina Fox:
Thank you for believing in our vision and for dreaming big with us. Thank you not only for agreeing to create this class, but for truly jumping in 100%, even to the point of entering our make-believe world to become a fictional talk show host and interview our characters. You are amazing. Thank you!

To Mr. Jason Crawford:
Thank you for bringing Sombre to life, makeup and all. Thank you for putting so much heart and energy into him, and for delivering the best-ever medieval insults. And thank you, thank you, *thank you* for the cover art for the book. We love it, and it is *so* much better than we even imagined it could be. Thank you so much for everything you've done in support of our book!

To Mr. Dustin Goolsby:
Thank you for becoming Alric, and for truly getting into his character. You brought our vision to life. Also, thank you for your hard work in creating additional products to go along with our book. We really appreciate every bit of your help and support.

To Mr. Craig Fertic:
Thank you for envisioning such a creative and beautiful way to truly make our book match the world it is from. Thank you for all of your hard work creating the products to go with our book to really make it stand out as something special. We really appreciate all of your work and your support of this project.

To Mrs. Julie Sanchez:
Thank you for being our online face of Atara, and allowing us to use your Facebook account to create Tara's real-world presence. Also, thank you for letting Gracie use your account to do all of our extra revision and discussion sessions outside of class. You are the coolest mom ever.

A Note from the Editor:

When I first presented the idea for a Collaborative Novel Writing class to Class Source's Director, I had no idea how things would go or whether I'd even get enough students to open the class. I only knew that I wanted to try it. We announced the class just before Winter Break, with the plan to start it at the beginning of the Spring Semester, just a few weeks away. On the first day of Spring semester classes, I still wasn't sure the class was going to go through. But at the last minute, one more registration came in. I had met the minimum requirements: I had 3 students.

Creating an entire novel in just one semester with only 3 students seemed like a daunting task. But I was determined to try.

What happened in the following few months was nothing short of amazing. We began from scratch. No characters, no plot, nothing. As I guided my three students – one high school junior, one high school sophomore, and one 7th grader – through brainstorming sessions, an entire world emerged. They created the premise. The characters. The plot. The backstory. An entire fictional dimension. They researched Canada, and the 1970s, and they built this story piece by piece, together.

Gracie, Lindy, Emily – it has been my honor to guide your writing process, to facilitate your discussions, and to witness your brilliant creative energy. It has been my privilege to watch you work tirelessly, both in class and out, writing, critiquing, rewriting, discussing, tweaking, revising, and writing some more. It has been my pleasure to be your editor, to read your work and to help you hone it. Your dedication to this project and your outstanding work ethic have far exceeded my expectations. You have done online discussions and weekend revisions and even video-chat brainstorming sessions with me, all to make this book great. And beyond that, you got everything to me by the deadline, even after we had to move it up by two weeks. That. Is. Amazing. But even more than how hard you worked, I have admired your character. I have witnessed all three of you give and receive constructive criticism with kindness and grace. You have opened yourselves up to be read and evaluated by me and by one another with the commitment to come to solutions that work for everyone, even when it meant changing your initial approach to something or rewriting an entire section of the book. From day one, you three acted as a team, determined to make this book the best that it could be, and to build one another up in the process. Thank you. You have made this class such a pleasure to teach, and I am honored to be both your instructor and your editor. *I am so proud of you.*

And to our readers – thank you for supporting our cause, and for purchasing this book. Not only will the proceeds go toward creating scholarships for Class Source students, but you have given these three students the gift of believing in their created world enough to enter it with them.

As their teacher, I want you to know that this means a lot to them.

As the editor, I simply want to say: Welcome to Beyaluna.

Sincerely,
Crystal Crawford, Editor and Class Source Instructor

Beyaluna Burns

Prologue

The kingdom echoes with screams. The perfect stone houses are crumbling and falling. The intricately made straw roofs release puffs of smoke, as if sending a distress signal. The doors, made from hours of careful workmanship and each with its own golden handle, are falling off their melted hinges. The large windows, rimmed with wooden flower boxes filled with roses and tulips, are withering and burning. The boxes fall off the windows, tripping those running panicked through the streets. The flowers smolder and send black ash into the air. The small market place, once filled with happy and content villagers, now burns like a match. The stone walls that kept the citizens safe are crumbling and falling. The pale blue castle, which has always been the pride of the kingdom – made with the help of Elves and adorned with towers covered in lovely gilded flowers – is standing within a small unburned area in the center of the city. Flames are steadily creeping toward it, and soldiers are running frantically in and out, trying to keep the fire at bay. All around the castle, sunlight and flame flash off the swords of the soldiers in battle defending the city. The shadow forces have invaded, and they are pressing toward the castle. The city's protections have failed. The once-gorgeous kingdom is burning.

Outside the walls of the city, two young women are running toward a small hill. The hill is far enough away that the screams from the city can no longer be heard, but it is close enough to still feel the heat of the flame. Aeryn holds her precious baby girl in her arms as she runs. She clutches her baby with the force of a mother's fear, and there is only one thought that can make her release her grip on her child: Alric. When they reach the top of the hill, tired and panting, Aeryn hands Atara the baby and extends her arms. Aeryn strains her outstretched arms and her face wrinkles in concentration. A bright flash and a small humming noise fill the air, and a shimmering blue disc appears a few inches from them. Atara reaches out to hand Aeryn the baby back, but Aeryn's gaze is locked on the burning city.

"If I'm not back before the fire spreads, take the baby through the portal," Aeryn commands.

"What? Wait!" Atara reaches out for Aeryn, but Aeryn is already running toward the city. "Aeryn! Come back!" Atara calls out.

"I can't leave Alric!" Aeryn yells, still running.

"He's not worth it!" Atara says, screaming as much as her body can support.

"He is my husband," Atara runs after her, and Aeryn spins to face her.

"Are you insane?!"

Aeryn pauses, and reaches for the baby, but Atara pulls back. The sting of betrayal etches in Aeryn's eyes. She reaches farther and takes her baby in her arms anyway, kisses her cheeks, hugs her against her chest. She whispers something to the baby and blinks away tears.

"Aeryn," Atara says, "if you go, you won't come back."

"I'll try." She gives the baby one last kiss, then shoves her into Atara's arms. Atara grabs her by instinct, and before she can respond, Aeryn is already running, her blonde hair flying in the wind.

"Aeryn, no! Wait!" she yells.

Aeryn turns for one moment, and Atara can see the pleading in her face. "Please, keep her safe!" she yells. And then she is running again.

Atara yells out countless times, but Aeryn keeps running. Atara watches until Aeryn's small figure disappears within the gates of the city, and then she waits. The small baby wails, wanting her mother. Atara rocks the infant in her arms. Hours creep by. The fire is spreading, and smoke is rising from the kingdom, filling the night sky. The baby has finally fallen asleep, and Atara sits silently on the hill, weeping with the baby in her arms. The fire reaches the grass, creeping

nearer and nearer to Atara. The ashes sting in her eyes. Atara
calls out to her friend one last time, her voice cracking.
"Aeryn, please hurry!"

The castle roars on fire. The screams are now loud
enough to be heard from the hill. The baby is still crying, the
ring of flame is spreading nearer and nearer the hill, and still
there is no sign of Aeryn. Atara rises and walks to the portal.
An ear-splitting scream pierces through the air. She knows
now, somehow, that there is no more point in waiting. Her
best friend, her queen, is gone. Hot tears fall down her cheeks.
No turning back. She takes one deep breath, then steps through
the swirling portal.

For a second Atara feels as if she is floating, then lands
roughly on hard ground, forcing herself not to cry. The baby
screams against her chest. Her long hair blows in the wind as
she sits up. She is in an alley near an abnormally large
building. The sign on the building reads Dormitory. She sighs
and holds the baby closer. Sad and a tiny bit afraid, she takes a
step away from the portal. It seals behind her. The ties she had
with the only world she knew are gone.

No, she thinks. She clutches Aeryn's baby closer still. *I
made a promise to my queen.* She tucks her grief away and stares
at the road in front of her. This isn't all new to her. Aeryn had
told her about this place, and where to go in case of
emergency.

Okay. Just stand here and yell "taxi." That's what she said.
As she stood there, Atara got lost in thought. Aeryn. Maybe,
just maybe, she'll reopen and come back through the portal…
no. *Keep your head on, Atara!* She walks to the corner and
screams "taxi" as loud as she can. After a few tries, a small
yellow carriage with the word Taxi painted on the side pulls
up. She walks toward the odd-shaped, horseless carriage, and
asks the man inside to take her to the nearest inn. He has a
small hat and a brown beard, and gives her an unfriendly
look. He tells her to sit down, and she simply nods and does

what she is told. Inside the taxi, Atara rocks the baby as she studies the man. She doesn't know what to do next. As the taxi travels, Atara gazes through the window at the stars flying by in the night sky. Maybe this new life won't be so bad, as long as she acts normal. She just has to study these odd people and act like them. Atara holds hope that one day she will return to her home and be reunited with her queen. She sees her friend's pleading face, as clear as if Aeryn is sitting in the taxi with her. Keep her safe, she hears the voice call. The baby cries once again, interrupting her thoughts. "Hush now," Atara says soothingly. "I'll take care of you, little Lucilla."

Chapter 1

"I can't believe it," Tara said as she tucked a lock of Luci's orange hair behind her ear, "my baby is really in college." Luci could see her eyes shining with potential tears.

"Please don't cry, Mom; it's not like I'm moving out of the country. It's only a thirty-minute drive from the house to my dorm." Luci did her best to reassure her mom that it would be okay, but that was easier said than done.

"At least let me help you carry these boxes up to the dorm," her mom said.

"I know this is just you trying to stay longer, but I'm not one to turn down an offer to help with all of these boxes," Luci replied.

Tara laughed but picked up a couple of boxes anyway.

On the way to her dorm, Luci finally got the chance to look around and couldn't help but smile at what she saw. Between all of the bright green shrubbery, she could see some of her new classmates. There were guys riding around on their skateboards and girls were lying around in the sun wearing their bell bottoms or granny skirts. There was even a group of people across the campus with a boom box, dancing around to AC/DC.

"This seems like a cool place. All of the kids look like they're having fun," Luci heard her mom say as they opened the door to the dorms that she would be living in for the next nine months.

"Yeah, I think I'll have fun here." Luci responded while she looked at the directory posted in the lobby. "Looks like room 234 is on the second floor, and the stairs are that way." Luci gestured to the right with a tilt of her head.

"232, 233, ah here it is; room 234." Luci leaned back to call to her mom. "It's right here. The door's open: I guess my roommate's here already."

"Oh, yay! Maybe I'll get to meet her after all," Tara said.

Luci opened the door the rest of the way and got a look at her room. There were two beds and two small closets, as well as two equally small desks. The only difference in the two sides of the room was that one was plain and the other already looked like someone lived there. There was a pair of purple roller skates at the end of the bed and the closet was bursting at the seam with clothes. Luci couldn't even see the beige walls behind all of the posters and pictures that were taped to them. There were posters for *Motley Crew, AC/DC, Mork and Mindy, The Brady Bunch,* and *Charlie's Angels.* There was a Rubik's cube on the desk and platform shoes strewn everywhere.

"So you must be my roommate." A voice sounded behind Luci and Tara. When they turned around, they saw a girl standing in the doorway. She was wearing a midi skirt with platform sandals and a crop top with a beaded belt hanging loose around her hips, and a flowery headband was holding back her long black hair that hung halfway down her back.

"I'm Violet," the girl said, extending her hand for Luci to shake.

"I'm Luci. That's my mom; she's just helping me carry all of my boxes up here." Luci set the boxes down on her bed and shook Violet's hand. Violet then reached over to shake Tara's hand.

"Please call me Tara," Tara said as she shook Violet's hand. "I'm going to go back downstairs and get the last couple of boxes. I'll be right back."

"I was just walking around the dorm and checking out where the bathrooms and everything were," Violet told Luci after Tara left the room. "I'm gonna go back and finish looking around the top two floors and let you unpack."

Luci started opening one of the boxes she had just carried into her room. When she opened it up, she was greeted with the familiar sight of all of her old fairy tale books. Ever since her mother read to her from one of them as a child, Luci had been fascinated with these fairy tales and myths that told of magic and happily-ever-afters. That was actually what she would be studying while she was in college: myths and fables. It seemed like a pretty useless degree, but if she was going to spend a couple of years in college, she was going to spend it studying something she genuinely loved.

Luci was carefully organizing her books on the shelf above her desk along with all of her textbooks when Tara walked back in.

"Here are your last couple of boxes, honey." She stepped into the room and set the boxes on the bed. "I can't believe this is really it. My baby girl is in college now. It seems like just yesterday you were in diapers."

"I get it, Mom," Luci said with an exaggerated sigh. "I'll miss you, too, but you knew this day was going to come eventually. If you leave now, then this week can get started and I'll see you again this weekend."

"I guess you're right. I'm just worried about you. Lucilla, promise me you will not go out tonight." Tara grabbed Luci by the shoulders and looked her in the eye as she said this.

Luci grabbed Tara by the shoulders and looked her in the eye just as Tara had done to her and said, "I won't."

"Promise me, Lucilla." Tara's voice held more intensity this time, telling Luci that her mother was serious.

"I promise," Luci told her mother, slightly startled by the sudden tension on Tara's face. "You don't need to worry about anything; you raised a fully independent daughter." Luci looked at her mother with nothing but love and admiration. She couldn't quite understand why her mother seemed to be so worked up about something so small.

"That's my girl." Tara drew Luci into a hug and planted a kiss on the top of her head. "I love you, Luci. Have fun."

"I love you too, mom. I'm sure I will have fun, but there's no need to worry about me. I'll make sure I stay safe and be responsible." Luci pulled back and looked at her mother, who once again had tears in her eyes.

"I know you will, princess." Tara gave Luci one last kiss on the top of her head before leaving the room and heading back to her car. Luci turned back to the boxes and resumed unpacking and trying to make the bland room feel a little more like home.

Once she finished up her side of the room, Luci took a step back to admire her handiwork. She had finished setting up her books and put up a few posters and pictures of her own, mostly of her favorite bands and movies, then of course a few pictures of her and her mom. When she backed up a little more, she accidently bumped into Violet's night table and a picture fell off. She knelt down to pick it up and she couldn't help but see what the picture was.

The gold frame held a picture of a much younger Violet and a man who looked a lot like her. Luci just assumed it was her father.

"He's dead, you know."

Luci whipped her head around to see Violet leaning against the doorframe.

"I am so sorry! I didn't mean to invade your privacy; I was just stepping back and bumped into your night table and it fell off. I'm sorry I'm such a spaz. I don't even know you, and here I am looking at your personal stuff." Luci quickly scrambled to put the picture back in its rightful place and step back over to her side of the room.

"It's alright, just chill, be cool. It's not a big deal and it's not exactly hidden; I mean, the picture was sitting right on my night table where anyone could see it. It's not a secret, either. He died a few years ago and I'm used to it by now." Violet walked over to her bed and picked up the picture. "I miss him sometimes, but then I know he wouldn't want me wasting my time missing him when I could be going out and conquering my fears. That was kind of his thing. He always said that you couldn't let fear rule you, you had to go out there and rule fear."

"He sounds like an awesome dad," Luci said from where she'd situated herself on her side of the room.

"He was the best," Violet said. She walked over and sat next to Luci on her bed. "What about your dad? What's he like?"

"Actually, mine is dead, too. It's not exactly a secret, either. He died when I was really little so I don't even remember him. I don't know how he died; my mom never wanted to talk about it so I didn't ask. I thought it must be painful for her to talk about losing the man she loved." Luci just shrugged it off. She'd told this story so many times that she didn't really feel anything when she told it anymore.

"Oh, I'm sorry. At least I got to spend some time with my dad," Violet said without looking at Luci. Then she turned toward Luci, looking very excited. "You know what? We need to go out tonight."

"I'd love to, but I just promised my mom that I wouldn't. We have classes tomorrow and we need to get some sleep," Luci said. She stood up and walked over to fiddle with her bookshelf.

"Oh, come on! I just told you that you shouldn't let fear control you but that you need to control fear, and you're just going to sit inside tonight? On the first night ever without parental supervision? Come on! Live a little! Let's go skating!" Violet ran over to the end of her bed and grabbed her roller skates for emphasis.

"I don't know. I promised my mom." Although Luci hated to admit it, Violet had a point. She'd always listened to her mother. And she wouldn't exactly be out partying or drinking, she'd just be skating and getting to know her new roommate.

"Come on, I dare you!" Violet said with a look of finality on her face.

"Fine! Fine, you talked me into it. I'll go skating." Luci threw her arms up in the air in exaggerated defeat.

"Bangin! I'm going to pick us out some outfits." With that, Violet threw open both closets and set off to work.

When Violet finished dressing herself and Luci, both girls stood in front of the mirror on the back of their door. "I actually kind of like it," Luci said to Violet.

"I'm going to ignore the fact that you said actually. I knew you'd like it." Violet said as she admired her own work in the mirror. Violet was dressed in a pair of hip huggers and a halter top with a tan leather jacket covering her bare shoulders, and the same beaded belt and head band as before. She had Luci in a peasant top and a pair of hot pants with some black tights. "I only wish I could do something with your hair," Violet added as she picked at Luci's orange hair.

"My hair is just fine, thank you." Luci jerked her head away and walked over to her closet to pick up her roller skates.

"It's nice, but it does clash with those eyes of yours," Violet said while picking up her own skates.

"Oh great, so now you're going to make fun of my eyes?" Luci asked. She had heard it all in her nineteen years.

"Not at all; they're sick, but you have to admit that bright purple doesn't exactly go with orange," Violet pointed out with confidence.

"I guess you're right, but I still don't think there's anything wrong with them. I happen to like that I have unique eyes and bright hair. It makes me stand out." Finally picking up her skates and bag, Luci asked Violet, "Are we going out or not?"

"Absolutely!" Violet squealed and opened the door.

"How are we getting there, anyway? Do you know the bus schedule?" Luci asked Violet in between dodging the guys riding through the halls on their skateboards.

"No way. My mom got me a love bug for graduation. It's parked right outside; bright yellow, you can't miss it," Violet told Luci. The girls walked down to the first floor and passed by a room with an open door. The girls in that room seemed to have decided to stay in tonight. One of the girls was using a portable hair dryer and the other girl was getting her nails painted.

"You're so lucky; my mom got me a new book for my graduation." It was a really nice book though. Tara had gotten Luci a leather-bound book of myths that was absolutely beautiful.

"Well, your mom lives in this country, so for you a car isn't a necessity, but mine doesn't and she didn't want me using public transit in a foreign country." Violet pushed the door open and the two girls made their way to Violet's yellow love bug.

"So you aren't from here, then? I didn't think you had a Canadian accent but I didn't want to make assumptions." Luci had come across quite a few different accents even just from where she lived.

"No. I'm from the States, but I'm not from any particular place; we moved around a lot." Violet opened up the driver's side door and leaned over to unlock the passenger side so Luci could get in. "I wanted to go somewhere new for college, but I didn't want to go to too different of a country and risk having to learn a whole new language." Violet pulled out onto the street and turned right towards the roller rink.

"That's actually really far out. I'd never be brave enough to move out of the country. I like studying adventure but I'm always too scared to actually go on one myself," Luci admitted.

"If I do anything this year, I hope it's that I'll make sure you never say that again. Life is meant to be lived, not cruised through." Violet looked Luci in the eye before looking back up and seeing that the traffic light was green.

Shortly after they passed through the stoplight, Violet turned left into the parking lot of the rink and the girls exited the car. "Let's go have some fun!" Violet exclaimed before running to the door. Luci quickly followed suit. Tonight she would live her life and not let it pass her by.

"Aren't you glad I talked you into coming out with me tonight?" Violet asked Luci. Violet was skating backwards so that she could talk to Luci at the same time.

"Actually, I am. Thank you." Luci held out her hand for Violet to hold so they could help each other slow down, making a silent agreement to go get some water.

"That'll be $2.42," The clerk at the concession stand said. "Thank you; come again," he said after they paid. The girls made their way through the sparse crowds, back to the floor.

"Hey cats, look at these two bunnies."

Luci and Violet turned around to see where the voice was coming from. A group of guys was about ten feet away, staring at the girls.

"Just keep walking; maybe they'll give up," Violet leaned over and whispered into Luci's ear. Luci nodded in response, listened to Violet, and kept walking.

"Where are you going, girls? We just got here." The guy tried again but the girls continued. "I asked you where you were going."

Before Luci could react, she was being pinned to the wall by one of the goons. When she looked to her right, she could see that Violet was in the same position.

"Please just leave us alone," Luci begged the man holding her against the wall by her shoulders.

"I don't think so, bunny," the man growled back. Luci got a whiff of his breath and she could tell that the man had obviously been drinking.

"Listen to her," Violet said from close to Luci. "Let us go, Casanova, and maybe we won't rat on you to the man."

"I'm not afraid of the man," The guy scoffed, "But I do know what I want."

Luci looked her assailant in the eyes and said in as steady a voice as she could muster, "Let me go." The man blinked a couple of times before surprising Luci completely and letting her go.

"What are you doing? Why did you let her go?" the man that seemed like the leader asked while Luci stood there stunned. *Why had he let her go when she asked, but not when she was fighting back against him?*

"I-I don't know why I just felt like I had to," the guy said, with a confused look on his face. Violet took this moment of confusion and got herself out from under the other man and told Luci to run.

The two girls ran out of the rink as quickly as possible and towards Violet's car.

"I am so sorry; I didn't think that would happen when I convinced you to go out tonight," Violet said.

"It's okay. I mean, it's not okay at all but it wasn't your fault; and it's just a part of living life, right?" Luci replied.

Violet looked at Luci and gave her a crooked smile.

"Right; you catch on fast." She smiled at Luci and told her to get in the car.

The girls were almost to the dorm when Luci said, "Wait! Pull over!"

Violet was confused and frightened, wondering if she'd hit something. "What is it? What's wrong?"

Luci quickly opened the door.

Violet yelled after her, "Where are you going?"

"On an adventure." Luci said with a smirk before she ran over to get a better look at what she'd seen. A flash of light had caught her attention, and Luci wanted to investigate. As she got closer, Luci saw the strange blue particles take a shape. It was like a shimmering curtain hanging in midair. Luci had never seen anything like it before. It was beautiful.

"Are you insane? You scared me half to death and made me pull over just so that you could act like a total spaz and stare at nothing?" Violet asked, suddenly appearing next to Luci.

"Nothing?" Luci asked gesturing to whatever it was that was in front of her, "You're telling me that you don't see this? At all?"

Violet had a confused look on her face but just shook her head. "No, I don't see anything because there's nothing there. Listen, your mom might have been a cheese eater when it came to not going out tonight but she was right about the fact that we have classes in the morning. We've got to get back to the dorms." Violet turned to walk away, mumbling to herself, "Of course I get stuck with the crazy roommate."

She turned back around to see if Luci was coming but she was still just standing there staring into space. Violet was about to walk back to her when Luci reached out in front of her and disappeared right in front of Violet.

"Luci?" Violet screamed, running over to where Luci had been. She was standing right where Luci was last standing when she felt a strong force pulling at her and she herself disappeared from the eyes of the other pedestrians walking by.

Chapter 2

In the green, flower-filled forest, a brown stag grazed. It plucked at the grass beneath itself until the path was eaten, then switched to another. Its white ears pricked up, and its cycle of eating halted when a large blue, swirling disc appeared high above the ground. The disc was like a mist, moving and barely there.

Violet and Luci plummeted out of the swirling disc, and landed hard on the forest floor. The disc that they fell from sucked into itself, then vanished altogether.

Frightened, the stag disappeared into the woods.

Violet groaned. *What the-?* She sprung up to a sitting position. "This is not good."

One second she was chasing Luci. The next? Golden-tipped trees swayed in the wind, their leaves glistening in the morning light. Anything below the trees was dark, the morning sun still not reaching below.

Violet stood, frantically scanning her surroundings. The leaves under her rustled. "Luci!" she panted. "Luci!" Panic lodged itself in her throat and choked her. Behind her, in soft brush Luci lay, totally unconscious. "Oh, my gosh! Luci!" Violet sprinted to her, and grabbed her shoulders. She dragged her onto leveler ground. Violet's hands slipped as she adjusted Luci's head onto her lap. Violet tensed. She looked down on her shaking hands, slick with red. Her stomach lurched.

"Oh, my gosh. Oh, my gosh." Violet escaped from her jacket and pressed it firmly into the back of Luci's head. "Don't die on me now, Canada."Luci stirred and coughed. Violet could breathe again. "Luci?" she whispered. "Luci," she said, louder this time. Luci's purple eyes were brighter in the morning sun, almost glowing, radiant. They were a light of their own.

Luci pulled herself up, Violet still holding her jacket to Luci's head. "Yeah- ahh." Her head pulsed like a drum beat, pounding, pounding, pounding with the flow of blood. The trees turned fuzzy, and her ears heard only static. Then her senses returned. Violet was staring at her with wide, green eyes "*Quelle? Ou`- ou` sommes-nous?*" Luci cringed and rubbed her temple while her left hand held the jacket over her wound.

Violet perked up. "What? If you want my help, you're going to have to speak English."

Luci's brows furrowed together. "What?"

Violet looked thoughtful for a moment before bringing a finger up to her lips, signaling for silence. "Shhhh! I hear something. Quick, get behind the brush."

"Hey, can you – ?"

"Yeah." Violet crouched next to Luci and heaved her up with her right arm for support.

Violet led Luci behind thick bushes. Through the bushes, Violet identified the rustling as a man walking towards them. His blue robes shone in the just-risen sunlight and made the golden embroidery sparkle. The man crouched with his basket, plucked a plant from the earth, and turned toward Luci and Violet's hiding place, looking just above them.

The girls were still. Violet kept her wide eyes trained on him through the leaves; Luci sat against a tree trunk, sweat rolling down her forehead in beads, eyes drooping.

The man rose from his crouch, and turned and walked in the direction he came.

Violet's shoulders relaxed. "Dude, I feel like I'm on *Star Wars*." Violet spoke normally now. "Luci – "

Violet shook Luci's shoulders. "Hey, stay awake."

"Je connais, I know," she mumbled.

Violet's green eyes fixated on Luci's purple. "Luci, you're the only friend I've got right now, and pretty much my only chance of survival. Any ideas on how to get out of this major pickle?"

"Follow him."

The sun had totally risen as Violet and Luci trekked through the woods. Luci was betting on the man having poor eyesight. Still, they kept back enough that if he did look back, the girls could be still, and all he would see was two specks. They had walked like this for thirty minutes, and Luci's bleeding had almost stopped. Violet's once soft and brown jacket was now soaked through with blood. "I loved that jacket," Violet said.

They hobbled along the roots and twisted plants. "Where do you think we are?" Luci said.

Violet tilted her head and took in her surroundings. The sun had risen now, and cast shadows from the gnarled roots and twisted plants. "It doesn't feel like Canada, that's for sure."

But where else could we be?

"Violet, look." The man they had been following entered into a clearing, then out of view. "We're going to get out of here."

In the clearing was a level pathway that bent to the right and out of view of surrounding trees, and wide enough for a group of people to travel.

"I think I can walk by myself now, Violet."

Violet loosened her grip. "You sure?"

"Sure." Luci held out Violet's bloodied jacket. "Here."

"Oh, um-"

"I'm kidding."

Violet eased herself out from under Luci's arms, and Luci stumbled to regain her footing, but Violet caught her. "Whoa, there. Liar," she said, teasing. "You banged your head pretty hard."

They walked like that for what seemed to be miles, with no end in sight. Luci struggled to keep her footing as they climbed uphill.

A tower jutted up beyond the green-leaved trees, and as they rounded the bend a full castle came into view. It rested on a hill, surrounded by a city enclosed with a giant wall. Luci was in awe.

"What is it?" Violet said.

"It's beautiful." The walls around the city were made of thick stone and taller than the mountain as they grew closer to it. Violet and Luci followed the trail. It widened until the sprouts of grass were taken over by dirt and dust. The road and the wall met at an iron gate tall enough for an elephant to squeeze under.

Soldiers in the battlements strode back and forth uniformly.

Violet stared up at them. "Hey! We're in a medical emergency. Mind letting us in?"

The guards turned to each other, then stared at Violet, almost curiously, then resumed their patrol.

The girls spoke at the same time.

"Something's not right here," Luci said.

"The nerve!" Violet said. "Look here!" The guards dismissed her entirely now. "I said – "

With each of Violet's retorts Luci's head throbbed. "Vi," Luci said, "let me."

Violet was taken aback, but quieted. Luci focused on projecting her voice, then said, "Please, we're lost. We have nowhere to go, and are in need of medical attention. Please, open the gates."

Then, amazingly, they heard the sound of chain chinking, and the iron bars rolled up. Luci and Violet were free to walk through.

Violet stuttered.

Luci shrugged, elated with herself. *Why did they listen to her instead of Violet? And yet, somehow, she had known that they would...*

"What was that?" Violet said, astonished.

"I don't know."

"Whatever it was — I'm cool with it."

The soldiers returned to their march.

Luci and Violet walked under the battlements and into a cobblestone courtyard. The street split off into three main streets. Luci and Violet decided to go straight ahead.

Houses and places of business lined the cobblestone pathway; in the cloudy sky the buildings were dull. The silence was eerie, and set Violet on edge. She pinched the inside of her mouth to keep calm. She glanced at Luci, who was pale in the shadows of the cloudy sky.

A few townspeople were out. The ones passing the girls on the street looked up at them, then ignored them. *Weird,* thought Luci.

"Let's find somewhere safe." Violet paused. Where was a place she could call safe? "Relatively safe," she corrected.

"Agreed."

They walked through the medieval city, alert until a horn sounded. Luci and Violet slowed.

"That doesn't sound good . . ." said Violet.

Door hinges creaked as people started to leave their houses and join Luci and Violet down the main street. Pretty soon hundreds of people packed into the narrow street.

The streets were congested as women and children and men came to a stop. Up ahead there were murmurings. Luci and Violet weaseled through the people until they could see clearly. Dark hooded guards faced the crowd in a large circle, crossbows down, but loaded. In the center of the circle was a wooden structure. A thick rope hung from the post that ended in a loop. "Oh my gosh," said Luci.

Another horn sounded, this one deeper and more sinister, and now that they were up close, louder.

Violet pushed her fingers into her ears. "I swear – "

In the center, two executioners hauled a woman onto the gallows. The wind swayed her scraggly hair across her face and gave her the appearance of a witch. The bigger man held the woman steady, while the smaller executioner stuffed the woman's head into a sack.

Luci watched intently. *What did this woman do to deserve death? And why was everyone here to see her execution?*

The executioners eased the woman's neck into the rope. The air was tense.

"I can't look," Violet said.

"Don't turn away."

Where had that come from?

"Don't close your eyes," the man said.

Luci stared straight ahead, but Violet didn't. She circled around, searching for whoever had spoken. Bodies were pressed up to bodies, all taller than Violet, standing on her tiptoes.

The executioner held the rope, ready to let the woman hang. The pulley was let go, and the woman fell under the wood.

A soldier's eyes landed on Violet. In a flash he jumped into the crowd and strode in Violet and Luci's direction. Luci's heart pounded in her ears. Luci saw that the soldiers didn't look entirely normal. They were more like a shadow. The three shadow soldiers advanced at a faster speed, passing through the bystanders who quickly moved to the side, creating a pathway for them.

A hand rested on Luci's shoulder. She turned to a man in a hooded cloak, his face hidden in the midday shadow.

"Come with me," he said. It was the same man from earlier. Violet had just seen the advancing shadow soldiers when she was pulled at the wrist by Luci. The shadow warriors were faster still through the crowd, but the two girls were out of their sight.

The man weaved through the parting crowd, beckoning the girls to trail after him. Energy pulsed through Luci's veins.

He led them into the cobblestoned streets. The sound of their feet hitting the ground echoed in the street.

Luci looked back. No one trailed them. Up ahead, the man slowed and disappeared into a wooden building. When Violet and Luci caught up, he stood in the doorframe and motioned for them to follow.

The girls ducked under the heading into a high ceilinged room, and floor creaked under them. Luci was soothed by the wall's and floor's dark wood, and was immediately calmed. Her head felt light.

Luci's ear rung as Violet slammed the door.

"So what was that about, mister?" Violet said.

The man in the cloak was behind the shop's counter, pumping water into cups, and behind him bottles of liquor rested on shelves shaped like x's, holding the bottles snuggly in their slot.

"Sit, please, and I swear to answer your questions."

"No," Violet said.

The man stopped pumping water.

"Look, dude," she said, her eyes piercing the stranger's, "I woke up in a forest today. Then, I walked into a barbaric fantasy land, where people get herded like cows and hanged for God knows what. Publicly. And who were those warriors *trying to kill us*? So – " Violet clenched her teeth together, " – could you tell us, please, *what the heck is going on here*?"

The man challenged her stare. "Are you finished?"

"Yes. I think so."

With the three cups in hand, he came from around the corner to one of the round tables. "Will you join me now, without the shouting?" he said as he shrugged his cloak off and onto the chair back.

"Sure. Start with your name; we'll go from there."

The three slid into their seats. Luci and Violet leaned towards the man, elbows on the table, eager like children.

Dizzy, Luci struggled to focus on the man's words.

"Alric," he said.

"I'm Violet."

Luci ran her fingertips along the wooden table's crevices in deep thought. She paused before saying, "Luci."

Curiosity flashed in Alric's eyes. "Luci. Is that a nickname?"

"Um, yeah. It's . . .short for Lucilla." *Weird*, she thought. *How could I not remember that for a second?*

Violet cut in. "What were the things chasing us? And why did they want us for dinner?"

Disgust and something else laced itself into Alric's words. "Shadow warriors, you mean. When the woman was hanged, you turned away, and they saw you. That's what I warned you about."

Violet's cheeks were warm. "Oh. But what's the big deal?"

"It is everything to the 'king' that his subjects behold their loved ones murdered for nothing more than wanting to be free from his rule. The executions go on this very hour."

"What do you mean by 'king?'" said Luci, copying his sarcastic inflection.

"Sombre is not the true king of Beyaluna. The city is only his by force. Decades ago, he and his shadow warriors stormed through the city gates, torches ablaze, lighting anything in their path." Alric fixed his blank gaze somewhere behind the girls. "It happened almost twenty years ago, but I can still see the torches bobbing, the screams of my people burned alive."

"That's horrible," Luci said.

Alric tilted his head up for Luci and Violet to see his pink splotchy scar running from under the right side of his neck to under his tunic. "A parting gift from Sombre before I fled," he said.

The silence stretched longer than Luci wanted it to. "Why are you telling us this?"

There was light in his eyes, as if he was waiting for her to ask this. "I am the true king of Beyaluna. I want my kingdom back, and my people want their freedom. Will you help me?"

Violet and Luci looked at each other.

"Sir, I don't think we can. We don't belong here. We – We're – " Luci struggled to find the right words. " – not from here. All we need is a way back. We can't help you."

"But you can. Have you not noticed your apparel?"

Luci looked down. What used to be jeans, Converse, and t-shirt was replaced by dark pants, boots, and a tunic. *What in the world?*

"Whoa," Violet said, totally excited.

"How did that happen?"

"I don't know the specifics of your powers, but I believe it is called glamour."

Luci leaned back in her chair and tried to take this in. "Hold on. Powers? This is ridiculous. I'm from *Canada*."

Alric leaned in. "How else do you explain your clothing?"

Luci was silent.

"That's why I need you. My theory is not only that you can change your clothing, but your appearance."

"How do you know this?"

"Your eyes gave it away. They're Elvish." That wasn't entirely false.

"Luci, you're bleeding again," said Violet.

Luci touched her fingers to the soft spot on her head and pulled it back red.

"This needs to be stitched up ASAP," Violet said. "Know any doctors?"

Alric got up and went through the other room and came back with a box. He laid it on the table and opened it. Its contents were scissors, twine, needle, and other medical supplies.

"Not around here. I'll have to do." He was expertly trained on how to stitch Luci's wound, but that didn't keep his hands from shaking. He hated operating on anyone, but he didn't voice it.

After cleaning the gash, he applied clove leaves to it and stitched it. Luci felt a tugging sensation, but otherwise no pain. Violet stood at the Bronze Pinn's window, watching as families returned to their everyday duties.

"So," Alric said. "You never answered me. Will you help free the people of Beyaluna?"

"If I did, how would I help?"

"Intelligence from the castle. You can sneak in relatively undetected and provide information for the rebellion. Over the years I have formed a militia. We plan to storm the castle from the inside out. But our chances of success are low without someone on the inside to let us in."

"I want to help," said Violet. "Tell me what to do and I'll do it. Luci, these people need us. How can we live with ourselves knowing we've abandoned them?"

Luci knew she was right. "Okay. I'll help. On the condition that I'm trained. I have no idea how to control my powers."

He gave her a confident smile. "I'll have it arranged."

Chapter 3

Luci sat at the bar, thinking over the past few hours. So much had happened in such a short time, and her life in Canada was beginning to feel farther and farther away. In less than one day, Luci had discovered the existence of an entire new world, found out she was part Elvish and – her mind was still straining to believe this one – had powers. It was a lot to take in.

It was also strange that the man in the blue cloak that Luci and Violet had followed out of the forest had known the girls were there. When Epp entered the Bronze Pinn, Violet gasped. In his blue cloak, Epp quickly explained his true purpose to draw them into the city, and therefore to Alric. "I sensed you," he told them.

"But how did you get out of the city?" Luci said.

He leaned in close. "Magic."

It was then that Luci knew Epp would be her trainer.

"I knew it," said Violet, just above a whisper. "I knew he was a magician."

Alric sat far off on the stairs in the corner with a shy grin. "Luci, come here."

Curious, Luci left Violet sitting in the bar with Epp, and followed Alric up the creaking stairs.

"I want to show you something," Alric said. He led her into his bedroom, leaving the door cracked. His room was tidy, the bed was made, and his chair was tucked under the desk in the corner. To the right of the room, in the center of the wall, was a full-length painting of a woman. She wore a soft green dress with golden trim around the sleeves and neckline; her hair was pulled back, half down. The pulled back part was braided and hung over her right shoulder. The rest fell in blonde waves to her waist.

Luci was in awe of her beauty. She felt familiar, but Luci couldn't find where she had seen her before.

"She was your wife, wasn't she?"

Alric's eyes were downcast. "Her name was Aeryn. I loved her."

They admired her together until Alric said, "Towards the bottom of the painting; do you see her feet?"

Luci strained her eyes. Sticking out of her emerald dress was a set of toes. "Yes. That's awesome." Luci was glad for the humorous distraction.

Alric laughed heartily. "She never really wore shoes."

Luci smiled at the painting fondly.

"She sounds lovely."

"She was. We had a daughter. She was an infant when she died in the raid."

"I bet she was just as beautiful as Aeryn."

"Yes." Alric's eyes shone with nostalgia and parental joy. His eyes locked onto Luci's. "She looked much like Aeryn, even as young as she was."

Alric spoke as if he were leading up to something. Luci hung on to his words.

"She was born with curly red hair. Soft like hers." He motioned to Aeryn.

Luci felt as if she was catching on. "What were her eyes like?"

"They were purple."

The air was sucked out of Luci's lungs. "What are you saying?"

He took in a heavy breath. "Luci, I don't believe my daughter died in the fires of Beyaluna."

Luci scoffed. "No. It's impossible."

"It is? Luci, you have the same name, the same eyes, the same hair as our daughter. Tell me you're not my daughter."

Luci shook her head. She couldn't deny it. The father she thought had abandoned her as a baby hadn't. *She* had left *him.*

Alric continued, "Aeryn must have arranged for you to be taken to safety, and the best way she could think to do that would be to send you through a portal. It is something all elves can do but it was also something that Aeryn was particularly good at."

Luci thought through the new discovery and realized something. "I think that's how I got here. Violet and I were driving and I saw something strange on the side of the road. When I went to go see what it was I guess I got too close and I ended up here."

"Of course!" Alric said. "Elven powers come to their peak in the 19th year, and you… you would be just 19. Your birthday was last month. I remember it every year; yours and Aeryn's, too. Hers is in the spring." He smiled sadly, then continued. "Elven powers flux the most during the first three months. You could have opened a portal by accident."

Luci nodded, then her eyes went wide. "Could *that* be why mom – I mean, Tara – acted so weird that night? She told me to stay in, and she seemed really… off."

"Yes," Alric said. "Atara is Elven, as well. She would have known."

Luci's head swam. Everything she knew about her life was a lie. Except… here was her true story, her real family, sitting right in front of her. She looked up at Alric's eager eyes. "Hi, Dad." Her voice broke off.

"Hi, Luci."

When Luci and Alric went downstairs, Luci slid into the chair next to Violet and explained the whole thing to her.

"So he's your–? No way!" She playfully punched Luci's shoulder.

"I can't really believe it either."

Chapter 4

"I need to stay with you. We need to talk about this," Luci protested after Alric told her that she and Violet needed to stay with Epp for the night.

"And I wish to talk to you, too; but that can wait. You must learn to use your powers to your advantage before you're caught in a situation where you might need them," Alric said.

"First of all, we don't even know for sure that I have powers. Second of all, even if I did have them, why would I ever need to use my powers? I've gone nineteen years without even knowing about any of this," Luci rebuked.

"Can't you see everything has changed now?" Alric questioned. "You aren't even in your own dimension. You need to know how to utilize your powers in case it's necessary that you need to use them."

"Again, why would I need to use them? I might never need to use them but I do need to get to know my father."

Alric could see that the mood of the conversation was about to change dramatically.

"I've never had a family and now I do, " Luci continued. "I don't want to miss out on the one opportunity I might have to get to know them." She could feel the tears stinging in her eyes before they came. She remembered the same look on her mother's face, just the day before, when she'd dropped her off. *Oh no, my mother.* If Luci had just listened to her in the first place she wouldn't be here. Then again, if her mother had told her about all of this instead of lying to her, maybe she wouldn't be so lost right now. Before Luci could get too lost in her own thoughts, she felt Alric's hand on her shoulder.

"I know; I had a family for a short while before I thought they were all dead. Now you've come back to me, and the last thing I want you to do is leave. But I also don't want to have to feel the pain of thinking I've lost you again. Please, Luci, learn to use your powers. At least then you'll be able to defend yourself."

When Alric put it that way, Luci could see a point in his argument. "Okay, I'll go and spend some time with Epp," Luci relented.

"Thank you, princess," Alric said before turning around and leaving the two girls without even knowing what he'd just done to Luci. "Princess" was once a loving nickname from her mother, but now she realized that it was something so much deeper. Now it was just a reminder to Luci that her entire life had been a lie.

"Are you girls ready to go?" The girls turned around and saw Epp limping out of The Bronze Pinn with his cane half hidden underneath of his blue and gold cloak.

"Yes, sir." Luci wiped the tears from her cheeks and stood straight up. "We're ready."

Violet put her hand on Luci's shoulder and gave it a comforting squeeze.

"There is no need for you two girls to call me 'sir.' If we are to spend quite a bit of time together, and I presume we are, you should call me by my name. Call me Epp." The old man didn't stop walking while he talked to the girls, but he waved a hand and signaled for them to follow.

"Okay, Epp, what am I supposed to do while you're training Luci? I don't have any powers to practice." Violet asked as they raced to catch up with the elderly wizard.

"Ah Violet, I have so much to teach you. Everyone has their own power, the difference being that some people have supernatural power and others have natural power," Epp said, still not looking at the girls.

"I think this old man has lost his mind," Violet whispered to Luci.

"I can guarantee you, Violet, that I am perfectly sound of mind."

Luci could hear the smirk in his voice. Violet turned to the other girl with a questioning look on her face and Luci only shrugged her shoulders.

"My house is not far. It is small but I have an extra room for you girls to stay in. There's only one small bathroom but it's inside. Many people don't have that luxury and haven't since after the fire," the elderly man informed the girls.

"That's really sad," Violet said as they reached the door of Epp's small house.

"It is far more than sad. It is a tragedy. We lost many good people in the attack on our beautiful kingdom. We had always lived in peace and we never even saw it coming until the horizon started burning and our home was turned into a furnace." Luci could see a ghost of the past lingering in Epp's eyes. "You two sit down over there; let me go hang up my coat and set my cane down."

Violet went to sit down on the palette of blankets Epp had pointed to and Luci sat in a chair next to the small wooden table in the center of the room. Since it didn't look like Luci wanted to talk, Violet looked around and took in her surroundings. Epp was right when he said his house was small. It looked like it might be just the four rooms but it was still bigger than their dorm room back home. The walls were wooden just like the front door, and in the main room there was the palette Violet was sitting on, the table that Luci's was sitting at with two chairs, and a wood-burning stove. There was a door in each back corner of the house that looked like they led to the bedrooms. Since Epp went into the one on the left, Violet assumed she and Luci would be staying in the one to the right.

"Sombre did this to all of these innocent people and he killed my mother. He tried to kill my father." Luci thought back to the ruins that now made up this once beautiful kingdom. *My kingdom*, Luci realized; *the kingdom that I was taken from, the one that was taken from me.*

Brought out of her reverie, Violet replied, "From everything I've heard about him, he sounds like an evil villain."

"You can allow him to be a villain or he can simply be a challenge we will overcome." Epp reappeared in the doorway from his bedroom to the living room. Looking at Luci he said, "With you here, we might stand a chance now. That is, if you decide you would like to use your powers to support our cause."

Both Epp and Violet looked at Luci expectantly,

"Let's just see if I can learn to use them first," Luci responded. "Then I'll decide."

"That is more than fair when asking so much of you," Epp said. "Let's get started with the training, shall we?" The wizard was now standing up straight with no visible sign of a limp and a small smile on his face. "First, we all have to sit on the floor. Before you can start learning how to use your power, you need to be able to control it. We do not want you taking off anybody's head the first time you attempt mind control."

"She has mind control?" Violet's eyes went wide in disbelief.

"Wait a second, hold up. I bet that's how I got that guy off of me at the skating rink," Luci said.

"I would bet money that is exactly what you did. You could sense you were in danger and your body reacted involuntarily," Epp explained. "You were extremely lucky you didn't harm anyone because you weren't focused. Now sit down on the ground here and close your eyes."

Luci got up out of the chair and sat cross legged on the floor. Violet sat next to Luci just the same. "So now we just close our eyes?" Violet asked.

"Not just," Epp said. "You close your eyes and think of something good. Think of a time when you were truly happy and felt loved."

Luci thought back through her life for a moment like Epp described. The best one she could think of was the first time her mother ever read her a fairy tale. She was lying in bed and Tara had just tucked her in. She walked over to the bookshelf and pulled out an embellished copy of a children's story book and told her about a princess that was lost. But the love of her family and her people brought her back home. Even though now the story meant something different, it was still one of the best memories Luci could think of.

"Once you have the memory, I want you to focus on it and think of a color. Find the color that goes with the memory, the first color that comes to mind when you think of that time in your life," Epp continued with his instruction.

"Gold." Violet said immediately.

"Very good, Violet; gold will be your safe place. When you need to focus, you will use your mind to drench the world around you with gold," Epp said. Luci could hear him smiling.

"Green. A dark forest green like the pine trees," Luci finally said.

"And that will be your safe place, princess. When attempting to control your abilities, you will surround yourself with that same forest green." Ignoring the title of princess, Luci opened her eyes to see Epp smiling like he was looking back on a fond memory of his own.

"What are you thinking about?" Luci asked cautiously.

"You're more like your mother than you know."

Luci was about to ask the old man what he was talking about when he continued.

"Her color was forest green as well. I thought it might be attributed to the fact that she was one of the Elven people. Perhaps that's why it's your color too."

"But she was raised in the forest," Luci points out, "so wouldn't it make sense that her color was green? That was the color of her home. I was raised in the city; why would my color be green?"

"Why do you have the same abilities as all of the Elven people? It's in your blood. I am sure you'll find that when you begin to tap into your unique abilities, you will begin to feel a draw to the forest. It's not something you can help. When your mother moved into the castle after marrying your father, he had a large greenhouse added to their wing because she was feeling homesick." Hearing the way Epp talked about her parents made Luci realize what she had been robbed of.

"You knew my mother." Those are the only words that Luci could think to say.

"Oh yes, I knew your mother and your adoptive mother as well. I taught both Aeryn and Atara how to use their powers just as I am about to teach you." Epp had a look of sadness clouding his face. "It was a tragedy when our kingdom burned; many families were broken apart, including mine, but it was a real tragedy that our kingdom lost our queen and our princess. Your mother wasn't just our queen though; she was a princess for the Elves. Although many people knew her, not many people knew Atara. I considered it a personal loss when I thought she was also lost in the fire. Knowing that she survived won't bring everybody else back, but it gives me hope; knowing that you survived will give this kingdom hope again."

Luci thought over the new information she had just been given. This was all so new to her but she could see that the old wizard had a point. She didn't know how she was going to do it, but she had to help these people. Maybe being their beacon of hope was how she could do that. "Okay, I want to help the revolution," Luci said. "What can I do?"

"Your mother would be so proud of your bravery," Epp said. "Right now the most important thing is for us to find out what Sombre is doing in his castle so that we can know how to handle him and where to strike."

"Everyone says I look just like my mother. Even if I can learn to glamour myself well enough to not be noticed, what am I supposed to do? Just knock on the front door and say, 'Hey I'm new to town and I want to see the king'?" Luci questioned.

"That is exactly what you're going to do. But first we need to train you to control your glamour so you can get in the front door without raising suspicion as to who you actually are." Epp said with a mischievous smile playing at his lips.

"What exactly can a glamour do? Will it really be enough?" Luci asked him.

"Are you ready to find out?" Epp asked her in return.

Luci wasn't too pleased with him answering her question with a question. "Of course I am," she said.

"Let us begin practice then," the old man said.

Chapter 5

"I know it's our best shot, and it was even my idea" Alric said, "but now I'm having second thought. Epp, are you certain there's no other way?   I just got my daughter back and I do not want to lose her again." He leaned forward in his chair, his eyes seeking out Epp's face.

"Alric, I want to do this," Luci interrupted. "Nobody has forced me to do this. These innocent people have suffered at the hands of this man long enough. Someone needs to do something and I will be that someone." For a brief moment in time the fire in Luci's eyes burned as brightly as her hair.

"Luci, this is not your fight. You should not have to be that person." Alric leaned over the table to where Luci sat and took her hands in his. "We have each other back now, Lucilla. Do you really want to risk losing our chance to finally be a family?"

"You know I don't, Alric. I'm so excited to finally get to meet my father and get to know him, but even though I don't know these people, I feel like I owe them this." Luci squeezed his hands and looked into his eyes.

"You do not owe them anything," Alric replied. "It's not your fault you were taken from here as a baby. Your mother arranged for Atara to protect you. I understand you feel a duty to these people, and that would make you a great leader one day, but you have to realize that they do not know you. Like me, they thought you were dead nineteen years ago."

"I owe them everything. Whether I grew up here or not, this place is my home, and in one way or another, I think I've always known that." Luci took her hands out of Alric's and began to worry her fingers. "This man who calls himself a king destroyed this kingdom and these people kept it alive even when they had no hope. They deserve someone who will fight for them."

"Luci you do not have to be that someone," Alric protested again. "We have people that are willing to fight for this cause. And even if you can glamour yoursElf, how are you going to get into the castle? Luci, we'll find another way. There is no reason that you should have to be in the front lines."

"I won't be on the front lines. If anything, I'll be the safest one of all of us. I can do this. Let me show you," Luci pleaded.

Luci opened the door from the back room into the hallway and motioned for Epp to follow her a few paces away. Violet stepped over to the table beside Alric.   "Alric," Epp began, his eyes showing a deep understanding. "I know you're concerned about your daughter, but this will benefit us and keep her safe. Sombre is not going to be happy if he finds out that a stranger has entered his kingdom without him knowing. Luci is going to go right up to the castle and knock on the door."

"That is a ludicrous idea. She cannot just go up to the front door," Alric said, shaking his head.

"That's what we thought, too," Violet interrupted.

"She *can*, Alric," Epp continued. "The more innocent and clueless she appears to be, the less threatening she will seem to Sombre. He is more likely to take her under his wing, and that is precisely what we are counting on."

Alric sat back in his chair with his arms crossed over his chest. "But – no offense, Lucilla – she's only had a short time to train. How can we be certain that her glamour will be strong enough? If it slipped, even for a moment… look at her, she looks exactly like her mother." Concern for his daughter contorted the old king's scarred face.

For a moment, Luci was lost, thinking that Alric had been referring to Tara, but then she realized that wasn't the case at all. Her father had been referring to her real mother.

"I know I look like my mother but do you honestly think that Sombre would recognize me after almost two decades? Do I really look that much like her?" Luci asked.

"Eerily so," Alric said. "The hair and the eyes are different, the stars know where you got those from, but everything else is an exact replica of her." A veil of sorrow clouded Alric's eyes and Luci knew that he was remembering the love he lost almost two decades ago.

"I wouldn't worry about that, Alric." Epp stepped into the conversation once again. "We stayed up all night practicing, and it seems that Lucilla has inherited her mother's gift for glamour. She had it mastered in only a few hours; the rest of the night she was simply experimenting with it."

"You have really mastered glamour already, Luci?" Alric asked, astonished.

"Yeah, I did. I told you I would do what I needed to do to help these people," Luci told her skeptical father.

"This is… only the most gifted Elves can master that so quickly. You truly are so much like your mother," Alric said.

"Show him what we practiced, Luci." Epp urged.

Luci pictured the image in her head. It was a girl that looked like her but there were some very obvious differences. Instead of orange hair, she had dark black hair. Luci could feel something in her change and she heard a sharp intake of breath from Alric. Her nose shifted to a slightly more button-shaped one. She imagined someone taking a magic eraser to her face and wiping the freckles away. She imagined herself shrinking and becoming a couple of inches shorter. Once she had the complete image in her head, she coated the world around her in green just like Epp taught her.

When she opened her eyes, Luci was greeted with two sets of wide eyes belonging to Alric and Violet, and one proud smile belonging to Epp, who said, "Excellent job Lucilla. You have done a wonderful job. It seems you are even more like your mother than any of us thought."

At the same time, Violet said, "I watched you do that all night and it still gives me the creeps."

Luci smiled, partly at her achievement and partly at Violet's comment. Her once-purple eyes were a deep blue.

"I can't believe it, Luci; you actually did it. If I hadn't seen it myself, I would not know that it was you." Alric said.

"Thank you," Luci replied. "I worked really hard on it. Do you think Sombre will recognize me now?"

"He will never recognize you now, Luci." Alric said. "Epp was right; you did an amazing job disguising yourself. Unless you give yourself away by saying the wrong thing, there's no way he'll recognize you."

"So can I go?" Luci asked her father.

"I'm still concerned about how you will explain to Sombre where you came from. People don't just show up in Beyaluna," Alric said.

"We have a solution for that," Epp said. "We thought the best story to tell would be a true one. Luci will tell him that she saw a shimmering veil on the side of the road and went to see what it was. Then she ended up here. Some people in town told her she must come see the king so she made her way to the castle. This way she can't be caught in a lie and it portrays her as a lost and confused little girl. How can he say no to that?"

There was something other than strategy in Epp's eyes now, something that Alric seemed to understand.

"How are we going to get her out of the castle?" Alric questioned.

"Girls, please leave the room for a moment," Epp told Luci and Violet.

"This is about me, and I want to hear it," Luci protested, crossing her arms over her chest.

"Leave the room, Lucilla; you will be told when the time is right," Epp said.

Before Luci could say anything else, Violet gripped her arm and led her back into the hallway.

"What was that for?" Luci demanded. "I thought you were on my side."

"I *am* on your side. If I've learned anything since being here, it's that everybody has secrets and sometimes it's best not to know them right away," Violet replied. "Plus, if we're out here, we can eavesdrop and they can't keep telling us to go outside."

Luci could see a smirk setting itself on Violet's lips and a wicked look in her eye.

"Good point."

The girls put their ears directly up to the thick wooden door.

"Can you hear anything?" Violet whispered to Luci.

"I can hear something like people talking, but I'm only getting a couple of words. What about you?"

"A few words," she repeated. "Wait, I think I hear something."

Muffled voices came from behind the door. "Prince… help… allies… Elves… Kirem."

"What on earth is a Kirem?" Violet asked.

Luci didn't care as much about what a Kirem was; she was more interested in the fact that it seemed Epp and Alric wanted to ally the revolution with the Elven kingdom. Luci's mother was an Elven princess. Were Alric and Epp going to tell the Elves about Luci? That was why she wasn't supposed to hear; they were going to use Luci as a way to convince the Elves to fight with them.

"You do not have to do this, Luci," Alric said again.

"Yes, I know, Alric. You've told me that more times than I could possibly count in the last two days. You may not think I have to do this, but I do. You have nothing to worry about. I have all of my stories straight and even you said you wouldn't be able to recognize me behind my glamour. I'll be fine." Luci had a surprising firmness in her voice.

"Well then, it seems as if you've made up your mind." Alric nodded his head. "Take care of yourself, princess, and be careful." He quickly pulled Luci into a hug and kissed the top of her head.

"Thank you, Alric." Luci told him as she pulled out of the hug. "You be careful, too," she said, turning to look at Violet. "I know you'll be okay, but we won't have each other to ground us anymore. Good luck."

"Good luck to you too, Luci," Violet replied. The two girls hugged before Luci pulled away again, took out her map, and started on the trail to the castle.

Luci approached the castle and her heart seized instantly. This castle was more daunting up close than it was far away. But Luci kept walking until she got to the front door. She took a deep breath and picked up the door knocker and tapped five times.

She waited a couple of minutes for someone to come and open the door. When no one came, she raised her hand to the knocker again just as the door opened. Luci jumped back slightly in surprise.

"What can I do to help you, ma'am?" The woman who opened the door seemed to be an elderly maid just younger than Epp. Her hair was a silver-gray color and her skin showed signs of a long and well-lived life.

"I need to see the king," Luci said, doing her best to keep her voice from shaking.

"I'm sorry, dear, but you have to schedule an audience with the king. Make an appointment and come back then. Have a good day." The maid gave Luci a small smile before beginning to shut the door in her face.

"No, please!" Luci pleaded. "I'm new here and I don't know how I got here. I need to talk to King Sombre." The maid's eyes opened wide and she looked around her.

"Come with me." She quickly let Luci in the door and ushered her down the hall. "You don't tell anyone who let you in, do you understand, girl? You can stay in one of the back rooms tonight and I will make you an audience with the king tomorrow. I don't know where you think you are but you have no idea what you have gotten yourself into." Alric and Epp were right, newcomers are rare in Beyaluna.

They reached a room that looked like it was in the back of the castle by the kitchens.

"You are to stay in here and do not let anyone see you. I will come find you and tell you when it is safe for you to come out. Do you understand me?"

"Yes ma'am," Luci told the woman.

"Good." The woman ushered Luci into the room and closed the door behind her.

Luci looked around the room. There was a bed, a nightstand, and a trunk at the end of the bed. There was another door on the other side of the room, so Luci went to see what it is only to find a small bathroom attached to the room. Well, that was one less thing she would have to worry about.

Luci sat on the bed and went over the plan in her head countless more times until she didn't hear people moving around anymore. When she could tell the silence was permanent and not just temporary, Luci stood up and made the two steps it took to look out her door. It was night time. Luci could tell because the sunlight that was hitting the tapestries when she first walked in had turned to moonlight.

The reflection of the moon cast a silver glow over the entire castle. Luci wandered the hall and saw one tapestry blowing as if being hit by a strong wind. None of the other tapestries were moving. She lifted it only to find a door hidden behind.

Even though she knew she shouldn't, Luci couldn't help from opening the door and entering the room. The large walls were lined floor to ceiling with bookshelves, each one completely filled with books. One wall is clear of any bookshelves but instead is occupied by a large stained glass window. *It's a library,* Luci thought to herself. She looked around at all the books and it seemed like it was just a bunch of journals. Luci pulled one down from the shelf and opened it to the first page. *Property of Aeryn Howell.* This was her mother's journal. Luci stood frozen until a voice snapped her out of her reverie.

"I don't know who you are, but I know you're not supposed to be here." Luci spun around to see a man standing in the doorway.

"I-I'm so sorry!" Luci started. She replaced the book on the shelf. "I'm new here, and I got lost, and these books are just so pretty…"

The man's face softened slightly. "Go on; get back to wherever you're supposed to be," he said.

"Oh, thank you so much." Luci let out a breath she'd been holding since he entered the room, and slipped quickly back out the door and down the hall to her room. She would have to be more careful in the future.

Chapter 6

Alric woke Violet with a small shake. She grumbled and rolled over, sticking her head under her pillow to shade her eyes from the blinding sun. Alric shook her again, this time harder. Violet sat up slowly, glaring at the man. He stood over her with a smile on his face. Violet stood up, yawning loudly. Her hair stood on end, clearly needing a brush.

"Get up, lass. We've got quite the busy day ahead," Alric told the young girl.

Violet raised her eyebrow, curious about why she had to wake up so early.

Alric told her to get up and go explore the camp. She nodded and walked over to the changing tent. An older woman stood up and greeted Violet, giving her some clothes and a hair brush made of animal hair. Violet thanked her and walked into the tent. Inside the enclosed space, there was a stump to sit on and a small bowl of water that acted as the mirror. Violet slipped on the clothes that were given to her and looked over into the bowl. She wore a gold-colored top paired with a brown jacket. A pair of brown pants covered her legs, keeping her warm. She slipped on her hairband, brushed her hair, and walked out of the tent. When no one was looking, Violet slipped a tiny apple off a tree and put it into her jacket pocket for breakfast. She looked around. The rebels walked around their camp slowly and unhappily. Not one was smiling, not even a hint of happiness or love. It felt like a cloud of gloom covered the camp, suffocating all good emotions. They all did their tasks without joy or energy. Some people were sharpening spears, some comforted a crying boy, and others were sobbing over loved ones lost to the shadow king's executions. Violet had enough of the shadow king. *Who does this cat think he is? He just thinks he can ruin people's lives without a second thought. Well, I'll second thought his face!* She thought angrily. Violet turned her head back to the small boy. Tears fell down his cheeks like waterfalls. She walked up to him, slowly but confidently. He stared at Violet as she squatted down and looked at him. His crying slowed down.

"What's the matter, sweetie?" Violet asked sympathetically. The boy sniffled and looked up at her.

"They took Mommy!" he cried out. "The meanie king took my mommy!" He sobbed even harder than before.

Violet pulled the young boy into an embrace. He hugged her back, still crying.

She looked at the boy sternly. "Don't worry," she told him, "We'll get her back, or die trying." She pulled him into another embrace and let him go.

The boy smiled and thanked her. He stopped crying and ran back to the people taking care of him.

One girl from the group approached Violet. "Thank you," she said.

Violet smiled and nodded. "Think nothing of it," she said as they took the little boy down to the lake to play.

"Wow, you're good, lass," a voice called out behind Violet.

She turned around to see Alric standing there, smiling.

"We could really use someone like you," he said.

Violet smiled back. Her white teeth sparkled in the sun like stars. "I'm not staying forever, but I can help for the time being," she replied.

Alric patted her softly on the back. "I know. But it is nice having an extra set of hands," he said.

Violet nodded and began to walk off.

"Wait! I forgot!" Alric called out, catching Violet's attention. "I need some help. We need to seek the help of the Elven Kingdom. They will be more than willing to help if you come along, I'm sure."

Violet stood there and thought for a few moments. "Alright, I'll come," she agreed. She thought it was nice to feel needed, especially since Luci had been getting a special amount of attention. Then she remembered something. "Oh yeah, did Luci make it?"

"Yes, not that long ago, lass," Alric informed her.

Violet smiled again, happy to know her friend was okay. She told Alric she'd meet him later and walked off to gather what she needed.

Violet looked around the camp a little more on her way. She stopped by a poor man who was calling out to the people passing him.

"Won't you help feed a poor man?" he called out. Everyone just kept walking, as gloomy as ever. She pulled out her small apple and handed it to him.

"Bless you!" he thanked her.

Violet watched as the man happily bit into the apple. She turned around and saw Epp's tent. *Might as well,* Violet decided. She walked over the old wizard to let him know of her and Alric's journey.

"Ah, Violet. I see you are doing well," Epp said.

"I am, Epp. How are you?" Violet asked. She purposefully left out *cat* or *dog*, knowing he didn't understand what those terms meant.

"I'm doing very well, Violet," he replied. "Good luck on your trip to the Elven Kingdom. Best you get going."

How he knew that, Violet didn't understand. She just shrugged it off and kept on moving throughout the small camp, then headed to the Bronze Pinn to pick up supplies. On her way over, she noticed a few children playing with flowers and little hand-made toys. The toys looked to be made out of wood scraps and cleaning rags. The children looked so content, as if everything was right with the world. She walked into the tavern, ready to get going on her journey. Violet told the bartender where she was going and what she needed. The young man handed her a sword, a water canteen, and a backpack filled with food. She thanked him and went down to the lake near her tent. She sat down to fill up her canteen with the fresh water that the lake contained. The sun's reflection bounced off the calm lake and into Violet's dark eyes. She squinted and looked up into the air. Not a single cloud was in the brightly lit sky. The sun shined unlike it had ever shined before. As Violet sat there, she began to wonder what the Elven Kingdom was like. She closed her eyes and imagined a whole kingdom up in the trees. It was safe and sound away from Sombre's dark reign. It had a roller rink, sky diving, color TVs, ice cream, soda, a drive-in movie theater, and... *Really Vi? There is no way those cats have that stuff,* she scolded herself. Only seconds later, Alric walked up to her. She turned around and smiled. He told her to grab her things, because it was time to leave the camp. She got up and squealed with excitement. Violet was off to see the Elves.

As they approached the forest, Violet was beginning to have second thoughts. All the trees were dead and twisted, and the tops of them were black as if they were scorched by the sun and were unable to bear leaves again. The ground was covered in dead leaves and twigs like a forest in a horror movie. Epp stood right in front of the woods, ready to see her and Alric off.

"May luck be on your side," Epp began.

"Because Sombre sure isn't!" Alric finished. The two old men laughed. They continued to talk with one another, discussing things like battle strategies, Luci, and the Elves. Violet paid no attention to them. She was far too busy staring at the dark forest. She thought she had heard a howl, which made things much worse. Alric turned to see her frozen.

"You don't have to go if you're scared, lass," he assured her. That, however, did catch her attention. She did not want to be called scared or afraid.

"What? Me? Scared? Nah, just so ready that I can't contain it, dog!" she said, confidence restored.

Alric rolled his eyes and turned around to continue talking to Epp.

Violet turned her head and saw a shadow move. Shivers went up her spine. Her confidence faded as soon as it came. *This forest has bad vibes,* Violet thought.

Alric said goodbye to Epp, and motioned to Violet to follow him. Violet waved goodbye to Epp and walked behind Alric into the dark, dank woods.

As they went into the forest, Violet's eyes darted left and right, watching out for danger. Her hand rested on the hilt of her sword. Violet was on edge, not trusting the forest. The trees began to block out the sun, causing long shadows to cast onto Violet and Alric as they trekked through the woods. Violet was not in her comfort zone. Alric just kept walking, ignoring her. Violet stepped on a twig, snapping it. Not realizing it was herself, Violet whipped out her sword ready to attack the supposed. Alric laughed, telling her that she was the one who had made the noise. She relaxed a little, but still didn't lower her sword.

"It's alright, lass. You can put it up," Alric told her.

Violet slipped the sword back through the sheath hanging from her brown belt. Alric raised his eyebrow at her.

"Sorry, just a little… cautious," Violet said, choosing her words carefully.

Alric nodded. "You know, all the trees are dead due to Sombre," Alric told Violet, trying to take her mind off of whatever might be scaring her.

"Ugh, you mean King Poop-Head?" Violet joked. Alric glared at her.

"We do not joke of him that way," Alric said soberly.

"Oh, sorry," Violet apologized, realizing she had crossed a boundary. They both fell silent, but only for a few moments.

"So lass, what's life like beyond the portal?" Alric asked.

Violet explained all about her life in Canada, what college she went to, and even her favorite color. She went on and on, until Alric interrupted her.

"Uh… question. What's a Canada?" Alric asked.

Suddenly the absurdity of the whole situation hit Violet. A few days ago she was beginning college. Now she was in a totally different world, had discovered her roommate had powers, and was walking through scary woods, helping a rebellion… this whole thing was surreal, like something from a movie. She had even gone through a portal. And now… *what's a Canada?* Violet lost herself. She began laughing like she'd never laughed before.

Alric just stared at her like she was crazy.

Violet tried her hardest to calm herself down. After a few deep breaths, she answered him.

"Canada is in North America," Violet began. "North America is one of the seven continents on Earth."

Alric looked at her and nodded like he understood what she said, which caused Violet to laugh even more.

"You sound very educated," he noted. "You seem to know what you're talking about."

"Thanks. I got an A+ in geography," she said, feeling proud of herself.

Alric looked at her funny. Violet rolled her eyes.

"Let me guess. What's geography?" Violet said sarcastically.

He nodded, looking eager to learn.

"It's a subject in school where they teach you about those continents I was telling you about," Violet said.

"Got it," Alric said.

Violet giggled slightly.

"So lass," Alric said, "tell me about your parents."

"Well, my mom is a professor at the University of Ontario. She teaches Language Arts," Violet proudly stated.

"What about your father?" Alric asked.

Violet quickly stared at her feet, not saying a single word. She hadn't really told anyone about this, or at least not how he died. Not even Luci. Alric looked at her with a confused face, until he got the hint.

"Touchy subject?" Alric realized. He continued to look at her, waiting for a response.

"A little bit," Violet replied, "He died when I was seven. Major car accident."

"Car?" Alric asked, trying to cheer her up with another silly question.

"It's like a carriage, but faster and no horses are attached," Violet replied.

Alric touched her shoulder, trying to make her feel better. Violet looked up at him and smiled. But the smile soon faded, causing silence to fall over them like a heavy blanket.

"He would always tell me, 'Be brave Violet, and you can conquer anything,'" she said, her voice cracking. Tears threatened to spill over.

"You know, my wife is gone," Alric said.

Violet turned her head towards him.

"Lost her a while ago to King Poop-Head," he said.

Violet smiled. "I'm sorry. Must be hard for you," she replied. "I know you said Luci looks just like her mom. Was their personality the same, too?"

"Oh, yes," Alric said with joy. "She was just as spunky and resistant as Luci."

"Wow. Sounds like me!" Violet noted, causing her and Alric to laugh.

"You *are* quite spunky, eh lass?" Alric agreed.

"Call me Violet. Or Vi," Violet told him.

Alric smiled and nodded. The two continued to laugh and joke.

"And then, he called out 'What are those?!'" Violet finished.

She and Alric both laughed like hyenas.

"That's too funny for me to handle!" Alric said, after calming himself down.

"You know, Luci's got a good dad," Violet smiled. *If only you were my dad. You'd rock.* Violet thought silently to him.

"That she does," Alric replied, causing Violet to giggle.

A flash of light hit her eyes when she looked forward. "Do you see that?" Violet pointed. Small lights could be seen in the distance. As they continued to walk, the lights got brighter and brighter. Small buildings began to take shape.

"We're getting close. We should be there soon. Any expectations?" Alric asked Violet.

"Not really," she replied. "Unless you count worry."

Alric smiled mischievously. "Then you're in for a treat." Alric said mysteriously.

Violet looked at him, just a little concerned. "It's not bad, is it?" she questioned.

"No, no. It's not bad. You'll see," Alric responded.

"Alright…" Violet said.

Alric walked more quickly, causing Violet to have to run to keep up with him. Concern filled her mind, causing her body to tense. He stopped in front of a tall bush, blocking the view. Violet paused with him. She saw a small smile appear on his lips.

"What's with the stop?" Violet asked.

"You'll see…" Alric said.

"Um… okay," Violet slowly said. More concern flooded into her. *What is the Elven Kingdom gonna be like?* Violet wondered.

"Are you ready?" Alric asked her.

She nodded.

He smiled and pushed the bush over. The light now hit them full blast.

Violet closed her eyes and looked away. Once her eyes adjusted to the extreme brightness, she opened them. She froze, staring at what stood in front of her. The Elven Kingdom was right there, and it was more beautiful than words could describe.

Chapter 7

Violet's eyes twinkled with wonder and amazement as she stared at the Elven Kingdom. The whole city was white, except the golden streets. The kingdom was alive with many Elves wandering the streets. Violet smiled and laughed. This place was truly amazing.

"Holy Cow, dude!" Violet exclaimed, "This place is better than a roller rink!"

Alric turned to look at her. He snorted. "You haven't seen anything yet," he said. He pulled Violet's arm, dragging her into the glorious city.

Violet looked around the magical kingdom as she and Alric walked down the glowing streets. Alric tapped her shoulder, causing her to look in his direction. She looked ahead and almost fainted with awe. A beautiful palace stood in front of the two travelers. It had five long spires shooting out of the main floor below them. A large balcony hung off of the second floor right above the front door. The castle was made out of a marble-like substance that reflected the sunlight onto the street. The front door was solid gold, or at least appeared to be. Roses and other flowers were planted around the castle, along with a few topiaries. *How rich is this dog?* Violet thought.

When she turned around, Alric was gone. Violet heard his voice to her left, and turned to look. Alric was talking to a tall brown-haired Elf. The Elf appeared to be kind, but Violet couldn't say anything for sure. His soft blue eyes looked like the lake back at the rebel's camping grounds. He was wearing clothes like Violet's, but his shirt was green and his jacket was a much more pale brown. He had a quiver slung over his shoulder and a bow in his hand. Violet stared at him, curious as to who he actually was. She began to walk over to Alric, when she tripped over an apple that fell from her backpack. The two turned their heads to look at her. Violet blushed, embarrassed about her awful first impression.

"Oh, yes," Alric began as he and the Elf walked over to Violet. "Kirem, this is Violet. She's from beyond the portal."

Kirem extended his hand to her.

Violet reached her hand out and allowed him to help her up. He had a strong grip, but not to where he was crushing her hand.

"Feel free to explore," Kirem told Violet, "We won't mind." His smile beamed like the castle in front of them did.

Violet smiled back, still blushing. "Thanks," she replied. She looked out towards the city. She looked left and right, wondering where to go. She took a few steps then turned back to look at Kirem.

"Got any maps?" Violet said, lost before she even started.

Alric laughed, but Kirem only smiled.

Alric told Violet to go and do something fun. He handed her some Elven currency, and Violet happily walked off.

Violet began to wander around the beautiful kingdom, gasping at everything she saw. She first stopped at the little market square. The Elves were calling out what they were selling. Violet looked at a small stand selling jewelry. She walked up to it, curious as to what Elves wear. The lovely jewelry had hand-carved wooden beads with floral designs. She picked out a cute bracelet, handed the girl some money, and went off to see what else was sold. The next stand she ran into was a fruit market. The fruit was odd-shaped, unlike anything Violet had ever seen. Some were red, some green, and some were colors Violet couldn't even name. She picked out a small gold fruit and took a bite. Her eyes immediately lit up. The fruit was so delicious that Violet could never find words for the amazing juicy fruit. She handed the Elf some money and grabbed a whole basket-full of her new favorite fruit. The next stop Violet made was a clothing store. As she walked in, the place was buzzing with eager Elves trying to find some clothing. The walls were painted a forest green with a trim of sky blue. The variety of clothing was incredible. There were dresses, skirts, pants, shirts, and even shoes. With her last bit of money, Violet picked out a pair of leather laceless shoes. She handed the clerk her money and walked out the door. Just as she did, she looked up and saw the sun shining in the bright blue sky.

As she walked towards the castle with her new shoes in her hand, a hand tapped her shoulder. Violet spun around to see a happy Alric standing behind her. He told her that the Elven King had offered them rooms in his castle. Violet's mind filled with excitement as Alric left her and went into the large castle. She soon followed him, and saw Kirem in fancy new white clothes, paired with a crown upon his head. Violet looked at him sideways, then walked up to her new friend.

"So, you're the king?" Violet questioned the Elf.

"Prince," Kirem corrected. "You saw me in my hunting clothes earlier. I was off in the forest looking for a delicious dinner for tonight."

"What's the occasion?" Violet asked.

"Well, you and Alric, I suppose," Kirem answered.

Violet smiled and looked all around the throne room she and Kirem stood in. "So, what's in your giant castle?" Violet wondered aloud.

Just as she did, Alric appeared. He patted her on the back and said hello.

Kirem looked at Violet and held out his hand. "Want a tour?" he asked.

Violet nodded and asked Alric if he wanted to join them on the tour. Alric smiled and gestured towards Kirem.

"I'm good. I have some old pals I need to catch up with," Alric answered. "Now, run along."

Violet nodded and grabbed Kirem's hand as he dragged her out of the throne room and into a small hallway.

Violet followed Kirem around his palace. He started in the kitchen, and let her sample some Elven cuisine. He next took Violet into the guard post up in the shortest spire. He allowed her to pick out a new sheath for her sword. She picked out a tan-colored one with a spiral design imprinted in dark brown flowing down the sheath. They climbed the stairs back down the spire and stopped at the second floor. Kirem took her into a small library filled with scrolls and hard-backed books. Violet pulled out a scroll from the bottom of a large stack in the center of the room. Unfortunately, she pulled out a load-bearing scroll, and caused the whole stack to fall down on top of her. Kirem laughed as she popped her head out of the stack like a weasel out of its burrow. She picked up a scroll and threw it at the laughing Elf. It hit him square on his forehead, knocking him over into another stack of scrolls. The scrolls fell on top of him, making Violet laugh. Kirem stood up and helped Violet stand and they walked out of the library, leaving a mess of scrolls behind them.

"Who's gonna clean up that scary mess?" Violet asked Kirem.

"You," Kirem replied, laughing to himself.

Violet lightly punched his arm, knocked his crown off, and called him a dork. Kirem didn't know what that meant, so he just kept laughing. Violet bent over and picked up his crown, placing it on his head crooked. Kirem straightened it, and Violet moved it again. He gave her a goofy smile and put the crown on Violet's head. The crown instantly fell over her eyes, blinding her. She laughed and pretended to march around like a prince, grabbing the rug she was standing on and placed it on her shoulders to be her cape.

"Look! I'm Prince Doofus!" Violet joked. She paraded around, dancing around silly. She ran into a wall, whacking her nose hard. She rubbed her nose where she hit it, groaning.

Kirem laughed and lifted the crown off her eyes. He stood there smiling, still holding the crown. They stared into each other's eyes for what seemed like forever.

I think I'm starting to like this fantasy world. Violet thought. She began to blush violently.

Kirem snapped out of the trance and looked out the window to avoid eye contact. He took his crown off of Violet and placed it back on his head. "It's getting dark," he pointed out, "You…I mean… I should probably take you to your bedroom."

Violet nodded, her blush finally disappearing. She followed Kirem down several hallways to get to her room. Halfway to Violet's room, Kirem reached for Violet's hand and held it tight. Violet blushed once again, this time not afraid of other people seeing her embarrassed. When the two finally got to Violet's room, Kirem let go of her hand. Violet looked at the door next to her room. She listened carefully to the noise coming from inside the room. The noise was extremely familiar.

"Alric always snores," Violet giggled.

Kirem nodded and laughed quietly. He opened the door and told Violet good night, then walked away to go finish his last tasks of the day before he slept in his room.

Violet looked at the lovely room she was standing in. The bed had a purple canopy hanging from the top of its golden frame, creating privacy for whoever slept in the bed. The purple curtains moved softly, blowing in the breeze of the open window they covered. The walls were the same glowing material as the exterior walls of the carefully made Elven palace. *This place is so bright, I could go blind!* Violet joked to herself. She changed out of her rebel clothing and into a pink night gown on her bed. It began to rain. The noise soothed her, making her more tired than she had ever been. Thoughts of Kirem floated around in her head as she slowly got into bed. Violet closed the purple curtains and blew out the candle. After Violet rested her eyes a tiny bit while lying in her beautiful bed, she fell fast asleep.

Violet woke up in a strange place she had never seen before. The trees had bright purple trunks and palm tree-shaped pink and orange leaves. The birds swam in a yellow pond while the fish flew in the snow-white sky. Violet looked at herself and almost screamed. Her skin was gold, her freckles disappeared, her once black hair now turned a deep purple color, and her clothing was different. She now wore a dress made of different patterns and materials sewn into a single long dress. *I always wanted to make a fashion statement, but this is NOT what I had in mind,* Violet thought. A small noise of crunching leaves could be heard right next to her. Her breathing quickened, making her heat beat faster. Violet froze when she felt something, or someone, breathe down her neck. The breathing noise got closer and closer to her ear, until Violet heard a faint whisper. She couldn't make out what the voice said, but she still was extremely frightened.

Suddenly, everything in the odd world was sucked into a hole like water into a drain. Violet screamed as everything was pulled in, including her. She tried her hardest to get out of the whirlpool that tried to eat her, but failed miserably. Just as she was being pulled into the middle of the world-destroying drain, she heard the same thing being whispered into her ear over and over again. She put her hands over her ears trying to block out the voice. Just as she finally fell into the void, Violet let out one last long and ear-piercing scream.

Violet woke up breathing heavily, completely drenched in sweat. She opened the closed curtains and looked outside the window. It was still dark, so Violet just closed the curtains and lay back down. She had a hard time going back to sleep after her nightmare. *No! I will not be scared!* Violet commanded herself. She closed her eyes and forced herself to try to sleep. No matter how hard Violet tried, she couldn't fall back asleep. She sat up, took a match, and lit the candle. Her eyes soon became heavy, so she closed the bed's curtains. After a little while, Violet managed to get herself on the verge of falling asleep. Just before she did, Violet opened the bed canopy and blew out the candle. Then, she fell fast asleep.

Chapter 8

Luci kicked off her blanket. It was scratchy, like all the other ones she'd pulled off the dormitory's shelves. She lied on her sleep mat, the only thing she could call hers in this blasted castle. A few feet next to her, a young girl slept. Her tangled hair splayed across her face like a spider's web.

Luci had slept next to her for the past few days. The girl, no older than twelve, would plop down on her hard mat after a long day's work, fast asleep before Luci and she could converse, which disappointed Luci because she wanted to form a friendship and alliance.

In the low candlelight, she could make out something under the girl's fingernails that looked like dried blood. Luci guessed that the girl worked as a seamstress and poked herself with the threading needle. The servants, or rather, slaves, as Luci had found out, were overworked and underfed, working from dawn to after dusk, only receiving a portion of cornmeal, soup, and water, once in the morning and once at night.

The women around her stirred. *Time to get up.* Within five minutes, all the women and girls had rolled their sleeping mats and blankets and put them in their cubbies across the room.

Luci was relieved when she was ordered by the head slave to serve in the kitchens that night. Tonight, the king hosted several lords from his court and across the lands, and a feast was prepared. For the Shadow King's feasts, Luci had been told, servants did not wear normal rags. Luci was given a light blue dress that was surprisingly soft to her skin. It dragged on the floor, but she didn't care so much. It was good to wear something clean.

Anxiety weaved its way into every last nerve of serving girl to cook in the kitchens. Luci and several other women from her dorm held bowls of sweet candies and chocolates, fruit, and cooked vegetables. They stood in a tight line, just outside the entrance to the dining hall, waiting to be summoned to bring the food out. Luci was first in that line. She clutched her bowl tightly.

Finally, a voice from the kitchens said, "Go! They're ready."

Luci carried her feet across the tile floor at a calm pace, careful not to trip on her dress. She left the hallway between the kitchens and the dining hall for a room big enough to host a multitude of people. Yellow firelight reflected off crystal chandeliers hanging from the painted ceiling, illuminating the counts and lords in the mostly bare room.

Luci fixated her walk to the far end of the table, where an empty space on the table was meant for her bowl. She glanced up to see that her spot was right in front of the Shadow King. Sombre, her mother's and countless others' murderer, was seated at the head of the table.

Luci had imagined him as cold and ruthless, but tonight he seemed pleased. He spoke with the two officials on his sides confidently.

Luci's stomach churned, and heat rose in her. How did this creature live with her mother's blood on his hands?

Just keep walking, she told herself. All this happened in a second. Her head remained low in false submission, and anger burst inside her as she neared the table. *Don't look him in the eyes.*

She couldn't stop herself. Maybe things were different in Beyaluna, so Luci took her chances. Even if it was disrespectful, she didn't care. Alric had described him as pure shadow — that's what he was, anyway, he had told her, but he looked more like a man to Luci.

His pale eyes pierced hers, and she snapped her head down. Heart racing, she left the bowl there, bowed quickly, and backed up against the cold wall next to another servant who she overlooked until she was right next to him. She most certainly would have chosen a place farther away if she had seen him.

"What do you think of him?" he said, just above a whisper.

"What?"

"The king," the servant said. "What do you think of him?"

Alarms in Luci's head went off. She had no idea who this man was or what his intentions were. She chose her words slowly. "He's the king. What else is there to think?"

He was silent, and Luci could just make out his light, shoulder length hair.

"Call me Caven."

"That's nice."

"You know, it is truly a wonder no one has seen through your glamour."

"How do you know about that?" Luci cursed herself. How could she have given that away? She struggled to maintain a straight face.

"Simple." His voice was hostile. "I observe. I get the upper hand. Now, I have a game I need you to play."

"I'm not playing any games."

"You will, because if you don't, I will expose you for who you are."

"Yeah? How exactly do you plan on doing that?"

He inclined his head toward Luci while staring straight ahead. "Because all it takes is the king's full attention to see through your glamour, then – " he ran his index finger across his neck.

How could she take what Caven said as truth? She didn't know the full extent of Sombre's discernment, so she played along. Maybe she could use this to her advantage. "What do you want?"

"Information — on a people group called the Rem."

"Okay. Where do I find it?"

Caven spoke in a hush and stared straight ahead on the feast. "The king has a personal library. Listen, and I'll tell you how to get there."

Caven's words echoed in Luci's mind. Like a spooked horse, she tiptoed down another dark corridor, hoping no shadow warriors frequented this place. The lit candle she held cast an eerie glow along the stone walls, and warmed her face already hot with anxiety.

Luci considered what would happen if she were caught. She imagined the king's dark, cursed fingers curling around her neck, and finally, after bringing his face so close to hers that she was under his hood, he would tighten his hold on her, and *snap*. A shiver rode up Luci's spine, and she shuddered. She banished the thought, and focused on walking.

"The entrance is behind a tapestry on the left." Luci looked around. Ahead, there was nothing but dark void, and on her sides, stone wall and . . .

Yes.

Luci looked up. The tapestry disappeared into darkness. She approached it and let its soft, heavy fabric rest in her one hand. She heaved it back, and this revealed a door, or, what used to be a door, for parts of a wood panel had been broken off and just the hinges remained. Curious, Luci started on the stairs, and for a moment she was relieved to be in a small space where light extended to all parts of her surroundings.

"Climb the tower, and you'll reach the king's personal library."

Out of breath and with a tight chest, Luci took her last uphill step. Her candle had melted almost halfway now. The door in front of her was wooden, like the one downstairs, and large pieces were breaking off from the middle, but the steel handle was still intact. Luci groaned at the enormity of the heavy door. She set the candle down on the cold floor, and pulled on the handle. She stood close to it and tugged. The door hinges squeaked as the door opened all the way. Luci guessed that the wall in front of her was actually a tapestry to conceal the door from the other side, like downstairs. She crawled underneath it, careful to not let the fire and fabric touch, and then stood up in the massive library.

Luci's eyes adjusted to the light, and the smell of dust and books stung her nostrils.

The light came from a window in the next room. Luci felt like she could live here for the rest of her life. The library was shaped like a dome with rounded walls. On her left, the white moonlight shone through slender oval windows as tall as a ship's foremast. Where the windows stopped, bookshelves began, separated only by a wood pillar spreading from the marble floor to the domed ceiling.

When her fascination dimmed, she remembered her true purpose. Find the information for Caven, or risk her identity and possibly the whole undercover operation.

On the ceiling were paintings. Luci recognized the ethereal character as an Elf. It was now that Luci remembered — this had been *Aeryn's* library.

The Elf floated alone on a white, shining background, eyes closed. From his fingers flew a blue light that extended across the ceiling.

A heavy weight found its way into Luci's head as she scanned for where to start her search. There must have been dozens of rows. Luci groaned. She walked up to the bookshelf in front of her and looked sideways at the title. How was it possible to find one book, and maybe not even a book, in a myriad of books?

Luci turned her head to read the title closest to her. It was thick and dusty. It read: *Whitesmoke: A History.* Intrigued, Luci pulled it off its shelf and opened to the first blank page, then the second. On the second it was inscribed to someone in a language Luci didn't understand. Next was the table of contents, which Luci skimmed over. *Introduction, Beginnings, Dynasties of Whitesmoke.* Luci turned to Dynasties of Whitesmoke. It gave a sort of family tree of the Neeves, Aeryn's family, and the Howells. It only extended to her parents' marriage. Luci was not there. She slammed the book in frustration, and then continued her search.

After what was hours, Luci's eyes lulled to a close. The wax in the candle she held dripped down to her skin. She gasped and righted the candle. After wiping the scalding wax on her tunic to get it off, which only spread the wax, she cursed in French, gave up for the night, and went down the spiral staircase to the servants' quarters.

The next day, she returned with renewed vigor. As she entered the library a chill reached her fingertips. A figure, seated in the chair close to the windows stood silently and without turning. It appeared large in its black cloak, and even taller in the moonlight's shadow, extending to her feet.

In a low, saturated way it spoke, and in an instant she knew it was him. "You're lost."

Luci's heart sped faster; she stayed silent. So it was a man then. *Run,* she chanted in her head. *Run! Down the stairs!* But she stood still, wide-eyed like a deer, ready to rush in a moment's notice.

He turned, irritated now, just as Luci started for the tapestry.

"Stop," he said, and she halted.

She gasped. Something like magnets attracting pulled her feet to the floor, and she froze. With clenched teeth she strained to lift the tapestry, but couldn't. The king glided forward. He stooped close to Luci's still face. His breath tickled her face.

Luci regained her sense of self then, and could feel her mind align with her actions. The king returned to his chair near the window.

"Strange," he said under his breath.

Released from Sombre's grip, Luci scurried to the door entrance. Instead, she found cold stone wall. Panicked, she raced down that aisle, searching for another way out.

"You will not find an exit," Sombre said, voice booming.

Her breath was jagged, her eyes wide. If she wasn't scared before, she was scared now. Fear heightened her senses, and she halted.

"Join me." It was not inviting. It was not friendly, and it didn't leave room for question. Luci obeyed, and sat opposite the king's equally ominous chair. It was like a lesser throne, with a high back and black cushions. Sombre crumbled into it.

Luci sat in a chair identical to Sombre's and found it hard to relax in. Was it the chair or her nerves, though? She stared at the end of Sombre's cloak, towards the brilliant oval windows that oversaw all of Beyaluna—anywhere to avoid his shadowy gaze. Sombre watched her with curiosity, and something else.

"I sense your confusion. And fear."

Luci was delirious. "What?" Luci swallowed. He had said something after that, and she missed it. She held a calm face, but her hands were quivering, scrunching her tunic.

The Shadow King's concentration did not waver. "I said, 'Why?'"

"You-you're the shadow king." *Wasn't it obvious? What's he getting at?* Feeling braver, she said in a small voice, "A thief, and a murderer." It was simple, yet the words carried such emotion, and Luci's throat held back a sob. Her despair turned to anger blooming in her chest, and she forced her breathing to calm. She challenged his gaze, and his eyes flickered to the windows. So maybe Luci did strike a chord in him. A small feeling of satisfaction glowed in her, then dulled as he spoke.

"Strong accusations for one so little."

His voice was like ice across Luci's skin. She wanted so badly to say, "You asked," but her voice was lost.

"You have Shadow in you," he said.

Luci's apprehension was overcome by curiosity. "Shadow?" Maybe he didn't sense her glamour after all.

"Yes. I have watched you, felt it in you — you have it, I'm certain. Would you like to control it?"

This is my chance! "What do you mean 'control?'"

"I mean for you to have total and complete power over your, well, powers."

"Then train me. Teach me how to control the Shadow in me." Excited, Luci said, "When do we start?"

"We start now."

Chapter 9

"Wake up." Violet heard a voice whisper to her and felt a nudge on her shoulder. "Ughmrumph." Violet grumbled to whoever was trying to wake her up.

"Violet, you need to wake up," Kirem said again. He shook Violet's shoulder in another attempt to wake her up.

"Kirem?" Violet whispered as she opened her eyes. "What are you doing?"

"I thought a pretty girl like you deserved to be woken up in a more civilized way than a large horn." Kirem smiled at a still half asleep Violet.

"That's very sweet of you, but what horn are you talking about?"

Kirem was about to answer her but was interrupted by the blood-curdling screech of a horn blaring in the distance. "That horn," he said, rubbing his ears trying to regain the hearing that the horn temporarily took away.

"Thank you for waking me up before that," Violet said. "I would not have been happy if that horn woke me up instead of a handsome Elven king." Violet blushed at her own straightforwardness.

"Well, like I said, I'm happy to wake up a beautiful girl such as you in a much more civilized manner. Unfortunately, now we cannot be so civilized. I must take you and Alric and train you in some of the basic techniques used in Elven fighting," Kirem said. His face was holding a grim expression.

"Well, I guess that's what we came here for after all," Violet replied. "We needed allies and part of that is being able to fight side by side." She watched his eyes widen.

"Violet, I was unaware that you had seen battle," Kirem said with a newfound respect for her.

"I haven't seen battle Kirem; at least not yet," Violet explained.

"But you speak as if you were a soldier who has returned from war. You understand the importance of unity."

Violet could see the gears spinning in Kirem's head as he tried to wrap his mind around the fact that she had never seen war.

"I haven't been in battle but I've read a lot of books and watched a lot of movies. Unity is an important part of them, too. You know, 'all for one and one for all.'" Violet laughed only to be greeted by the face of a very confused Kirem. "You have no idea what I'm talking about, do you?" she asked.

"I know of books," Kirem said. "The Elves think it very important to keep a written record of our history, but I have never heard of these movies you speak of. Though I think I might enjoy the one you say includes, 'all for one and one for all.' It sounds as if a great soldier wrote that."

Sometimes Violet forgot that she was in a different dimension and that here movies didn't exist, let alone *The Three Musketeers*.

"That quote was from *The Three Musketeers*. Where I'm from it's a book and a movie." Violet suddenly became homesick. "Maybe one day I'll be able to share it with you."

"I look forward to that day, Violet," Kirem said with a weary smile on his face. "But for now, we have to go and make sure Alric is awake so that we can begin training."

"Okay, sounds like a plan." Violet said, plastering a smile on her face and pretending that everything was okay. If she pretended well enough, maybe it would be true.

"I hate that horn," Alric grumbled on their way out into the training field.

"That is the point of the horn," Kirem said. "It is very effective in waking people up."

Violet could have sworn she saw the flash of a smile pass across Kirem's lips.

"I guess that part is true," Alric said.

"When we get to the field, I will teach you both how to fight with some of the weapons our people use," Kirem explained. "Even though we have lived in peace for many years, we believe the ability to fight well should never be lost. You never know when someone might decide to attack." The king glanced at Alric with a look that can only be exchanged by people with a shared tragedy.

"You and your people are onto something. Knowing how to defend yourself and your kingdom can come in handy," Alric responded.

It was right in this moment that Violet fully realized just how deep Alric and Kirem's friendship ran. They had both known loss and had mourned together. Now Luci had given both kingdoms hope for a better life and both men were seeing the light at the end of the tunnel.

Their small group made their way through the last cluster of trees before entering a clearing. Violet found it hard to believe that a place so beautiful was where they would be learning new ways to harm people. The sun shone through the leaves of the trees, casting a gold and green light on the space. The grass was bright as if it had been lit from behind, but it was only from the sunlight shining directly on it. Scattered across the meadow were small dandelions and colorful flowers that would make even the saddest person smile.

"My people prefer to fight with simpler weapons," Kirem began, standing in the middle of the field. The sun bounced off of his brown hair, making it look rich like chocolate and making the silver glow like a halo around his head. "Swords, spears, and crossbows are much easier to replicate on short notice when necessary." He walked over to the edge of the field to a large trunk and unlocked it.

"Alric, I know you prefer your crossbow so I will give that one to Violet. The purpose of today is to learn to fight with what you are uncomfortable with and to be comfortable with everything." Kirem lifted a crossbow and a small quiver of arrows out of the trunk and walked them over to Violet, who was just standing to the side, listening and taking in everything she could. "Wait here and I will show you how to use it," he told her with a small smile.

"I also know you are very familiar with the sword, which is why you will be learning to fight with a spear," Kirem told Alric. He leaned down over the trunk and pulled out a long spear before walking it over to Alric, who was standing only a few feet away from Violet.

"What use is a spear going to be in this battle?" Alric asked the Elven king. "It cannot be used long range and it cannot be easily wielded in short range either." He rotated the spear in his hands, inspecting it.

"You would be surprised just how versatile the spear can be when you know how to use it correctly," Kirem replied. "Violet, I am going to work with you first since I have Alric here to help me teach."

"Okay," Violet said, "show me how to use this thing." She slung the quiver over her shoulder and held up the bow.

"Rest the back of the crossbow on your shoulder," Kirem told her. He held the back and propped it up on her shoulder for her, moving to stand behind her and look over her shoulder. "Just like that," He said with a smile. "Now load the arrow by placing the bow string into the notch at the end." Kirem held her wrist lightly and gently guided Violet's hand in the movements he had just described. "Excellent, now pull the bow string back until it clicks into place."

Violet did as she was told and she immediately heard the click of the bow string locking into place.

Kirem ran his hands along Violet's arms, adjusting her stance. A shiver traveled down Violet's back at the delicate contact and she immediately blushed at her reaction.

"Stand like this, aim at the target, take a deep breath, and pull the trigger," Kirem said softly, since he was standing right behind her.

Violet followed Kirem's instructions and aimed at the target across the field. Once she felt like she was comfortable with where she thought the arrow would go, Violet took a deep breath and as she exhaled, she pulled the trigger. The arrow flew to the target and hit on the very outer edge.

"A little off, but you hit the target and that's a great start," Kirem praised her.

"But I just barely hit it," Violet contradicted him. "If I need to shoot at someone, almost hitting them isn't going to save me."

"You show potential, Violet," Kirem reassured her. "I am almost positive that by the end of today, you will be striking the bull's-eye the majority of the time."

"That is enough, love birds," Alric interrupted.

Violet blushed red again and Kirem choked on a cough.

"Kirem, I need to learn how to use this spear," Alric continued.

"You are right, Alric," Kirem said. He walked over to Alric and took the spear from him. "When it comes to a spear, it works best to be on the defensive. You use the smooth handle as you would a staff to defend yourself from offensive attacks. The end is sharpened to a point and can be used as a blade on each side. That's what you can use in an offensive attack of your own. Many people think of a spear and think it should be used in long range combat by throwing it, but it works much better in close quarters. The good thing about a spear is that you can defend yourself with the handle and use the end as you would a dagger. You just have to be a little creative with it." He showed Alric a few different maneuvers to practice on the dummy standing by the trunk.

For the rest of the day, Kirem worked one-on-one with both Alric and Violet and taught them both how to properly use their weapons. Kirem was right; by the time the sun was going down and they were about to go back to the castle, Violet was hitting the bull's-eye almost every time. Alric had even come to love working with his spear and figuring out new ways to move with it.

"I think you two are prepped enough to be able to fight alongside our warriors," Kirem said with a hint of self-satisfaction that he had definitely earned. In a day's time, the Elven king had taught Violet how to accurately fire a crossbow and Alric how to efficiently fight using a spear. "It is dark now. I think we should all go back to the castle and eat dinner before getting a good night's rest. From now on, we will not know when the next opportunity for that will be."

As the sun set beyond the trees, the trio made their way through the hidden path in the forest back to the castle. The air was crisp and the stars were bright. The moon was fat and shining brightly above them. Violet could hear the leaves on the trees rustling in the wind and the owls calling out from somewhere hidden.

When they got back to the castle, Violet, Alric, and Kirem went to their respective rooms to shower and change clothes before meeting in the small dining room for their dinner. Violet changed into some of the clothes that were left for her, a soft white shirt, some loose black drawstring pants, and a light brown sweater.

Barefoot, Violet walked down the hall past a couple of doors and saw the men already sitting at the table waiting on the food to be brought out.

"Hello, Violet." Kirem stopped mid-sentence and stood up when she entered the room.

"You can sit down, Kirem; you don't have to stand up," Violet told him.

Alric watched them both with a look of half knowing and half confusion.

"Oh, well, please sit down." Kirem pulled another chair out for Violet before sitting back down into his own.

"We were just discussing our game plan from here," Alric said, trying to catch Violet up. "Now that the Elves have agreed to fight with us and we know that we can fight alongside of them, we need to get Luci out of Sombre's castle before we begin our attack. She is already in danger just being there now; there is no way I am going to let her stay there while we attack," Alric announced with authority.

"How exactly are you planning on getting her out of his castle? What if she has been kept prisoner?" Kirem asked him.

"Against my better judgment, I am assuming that Sombre would not immediately imprison someone who accidently found their way to Beyaluna. I would think that he would want to question her and figure out how she got here first, so that he could seal up the pathway that she took. He would not want any more mysterious strangers showing up in 'his kingdom.' It would be too big of a security risk," Alric explained to them. Kirem seemed to understand exactly what Alric was talking about, but Violet still had to think about it for a moment. She couldn't help but feel a little out of place seeing these two old friends talk to each other and never skip a beat.

"That makes sense, Alric, but that still leaves my main question unanswered. How exactly do you plan on getting her out?" Kirem asked again.

"That is where I will need your help, Kirem," Alric said. "You are the only person here with a glamour that I would trust enough to ask you to go get my daughter."

"Alric – " Kirem started.

"Please, Kirem. I know that you want her back safe and sound almost as much as I do and I can only say that with certainty about you." Alric looked at Kirem with pleading eyes that somehow still didn't show weakness.

Kirem stayed still staring at Alric before letting out an audible sigh and saying, "Okay, what do I need to do?"

Chapter 10

Kirem stepped out of his castle and into the dark of night. Violet, who was standing just inside of the doorway, waved him goodbye. Kirem smiled at her and waved back. He pulled up the hood of his cloak and ran into the surrounding forest. Once off of castle grounds, Kirem finally picked up some more speed and he began to run towards Beyaluna as fast as he could. Elves were light on their feet, so if Kirem could keep this speed, he thought he would make it to the castle just before dawn. He sprinted through the dense forests. The woods would be his best bet to sneak into Beyaluna without anyone noticing.

As he ran, Kirem could feel the chilling night air sting his cheeks and he could hear the leaves crunch beneath his feet. He didn't know how long he had been running when he saw the moonlight reflecting off of the castle in the distance. Kirem paused and took a moment to rest. He took off his cloak and used his glamour to change into his arranged disguise. Black hair. Black eyes. Pale skin. Plain black clothes. Completely ordinary and unmemorable. Once he was disguised, Kirem stood up. He moved stealthily through the streets surrounding the castle and then dropped to his knees to creep closer to the landscaped boundary of the castle gardens. The gardens were the closest he could get without having to sneak past guards. He would need to watch a while from there to determine how best to make his way into the castle. Crouching, he pushed aside a bush and saw a girl just a few feet away, touching a magnolia gently. She looked exactly like the girl Alric had described. He had found Luci.

Luci walked out of the door and into the garden behind Sombre's castle. She looked up at the large moon and sighed. She could see why this place was called Beyaluna. The moon was always shining brightly, illuminating the night. She thought back to the night sh and Violet fell through the portal.

84

Back to before she even knew Beyaluna existed, let alone what their moon looked like. Before she had a complete family and before she was Beyaluna's long lost princess. Back in Canada, Luci felt out of place, but she was still happy. Here, she felt like she belonged, but she wasn't so sure if she was happy. A rustle in the bushes startled Luci and brought her out of her reverie. She looked over but saw nothing. *Probably a small animal*, she thought.

Looking a little to her left, Luci saw a patch of magnolias. She smiled as she bent down to get a closer look. The one Luci saw was a pale orange with light pink tips. It reminded her of the small plant she used to keep when she was very little. Magnolias were Luci's favorite. After all, it was what her mother chose for her middle name. The bushes moved again, this time revealing a man who looked like one of Sombre's servants. Luci put on a plastic smile, trying to look as if she belonged there.

"Luci, don't worry; I am not one of Sombre's minions. Alric sent me. They're ready for you to come back now," he said. Luci was shocked when the servant spoke of Alric, but her curiosity took over and she followed him.

"How do you know about Alric?" Luci questioned the servant. Once they were out of the garden, the man began to transform just like Luci had earlier. He was now a normal man with pointy ears. *Oh... he's an Elf!* Luci realized. With all the fairy tales Luci had read, the ears were a dead giveaway.

"My name is Kirem," he told her, "I am a friend of Alric and Violet." Luci smiled and nodded. Kirem didn't know how happy he made her just by mentioning Violet. Luci was beyond grateful that Violet was still alright.

"I hope to be a friend of yours one day as well Luci," Kirem continued, "but that's something that can be saved for when we get back to the castle."

"Castle?" Luci questioned. "You mean Sombre's castle? If Alric needs me back, why would we go in there?"

"No, we are going to my castle; the one in Whitesmoke. It is usually at least a day's journey away, but since I am an Elf and you are half Elf, we should be able to make it there in a few hours if we run." Kirem said matter-of-factly.

"If we run?" Luci asked him. "You're telling me that you plan to run all the way to Whitesmoke within a couple of hours?"

"We Elves are very light on our feet. If you put our mind to it, you can run all the way there," Kirem explained to her. "I do not know how it will affect you because you are only half Elf but you should be able to make it."

"And if I can't?" Luci asked.

"If you cannot make it, I will carry you the rest of the way."

Luci raised a brow at him.

"We are also very strong. It will be no problem to carry you, Luci."

She took a moment to process all of this new information. "Okay," she said. "Let's start running."

The feeling was exhilarating. Luci had run before but never quite like this. The cool air burned her cheeks and felt cleansing as it entered her lungs. The entire way she struggled to keep up with Kirem, but she managed to keep her dignity and didn't have to ask him to carry her.

As soon as they get to Kirem's castle in Whitesmoke, Luci was met with a force running into her. "Thank goodness you're okay!" Violet screamed, with her arms locked around Luci's neck.

"Of course I'm okay, Vi. I'm glad you're okay." Luci pried her friend off of her and looked her in the eyes. "I don't know what I would've done if you had gotten hurt and it was all my fault for dragging us into this mess."

"I did just as much dragging as you did, Canada."

Luci laughed at the nickname Violet seems to be sticking to.

"Now you need to come inside, shower, get some fresh clothes, and drink some hot chocolate," Violet said.

"That sounds so nice." Luci said with a sigh of relief as Violet led her up the massive staircase and into a generously-sized suite that she would get all to herself.

When Luci came out of the bathroom, now freshly cleaned and wearing a grey shirt and some baggy black pants, she saw Kirem sitting in a chair in the corner of the room. "Ahh! Tu m`as fait peur!" Luci clutched at her chest, feeling her heart race.

"What?" Kirem questions with his eyebrows furrowed together.

"Sorry, just ignore that. I've been speaking French lately when I'm caught off guard." Luci shook her head as if she could shake the confusion away, "What are you doing in here?"

"I must admit I was not completely honest with you earlier, Luci." Kirem confessed.

"What are you talking about?" Luci asked him while she walked over to sit on the gigantic bed sitting in the middle of the room.

"I am more than just a friend to Alric, and I hope to be more than just a friend to you," he said bluntly.

"That's really flattering, don't get me wrong, but I just met you" Luci said, weary of the odd turn this conversation seems to have taken.

"I am unsure of what you're thinking but it seems you have taken me the wrong way," he explained. "Your mother and I were cousins. My father and her father were brothers." The reality of what Kirem was talking about hit Luci like a ton of bricks. "I guess that makes us cousins, too." Kirem continued. "I think we are, anyway. Now you have come back to both Beyaluna and Whitesmoke. I hope that when all of this is over, the two of us can get to know each other better. Maybe even become like family for one another," Kirem told her with a mix of sorrow and hope in his eyes.

"I would like that very much," That was all Luci could say. A week ago it was just her and her mom. Now she had a father and apparently a cousin.

"Well," Kirem stood up and smoothed down his coat. "I am glad we could talk about this. I thought you ought to know. I will let you get some sleep. You have had an exhausting day and the next couple of days will not be much different."

"You're right," Luci agreed. "Good night, Kirem."

"Good night, princess Lucilla." With that, he opened the door and stepped out into the hall quietly, shutting the door behind him. That was all Luci needed to lie down under the warm blankets and immediately fall asleep.

Violet was sitting in one of the large chairs at the dining room table, waiting patiently for Kirem to walk through the doors while she sipped her own cup of hot chocolate. She looked away from the door for a moment to take another sip when it opened. She looked up to see Kirem peeking in to say hi. Violet set down her cup and rushed towards the prince. She brought him into a tight embrace and felt his face physically heat up in a blush.

He followed Violet back to the table and sat down next to her. One of the servants quickly brought him a cup of hot chocolate for himself. "Thank you," he told the woman before she bowed her head and turned to walk back to the kitchens. "I believe Luci is asleep," he told Violet. "I stepped into her room and the two of us had a nice talk. I believe she genuinely wants to get to know one another." He can't hide the smile that creeps across his face as he says it.

"That's awesome, Kirem! You two can be there for each other. I know all of us are going to need somebody by the time everything is over," Violet told him. She inched her hand across the table and her fingers brushed against his gently.

The doors to the dining room creaked open and Violet quickly removed her hand from Kirem's. Alric stepped into the room slowly, "Could not sleep. Are you two preparing for the battle?" he asked.

"We were actually just speaking of Luci's return." Just then the door creaked again and Luci walked in.

"I was asleep," she said, "but then I woke up and thought I should come see where everyone was." There were dark circles ringing her once-bright eyes and her posture suggested fatigue. She walked over to the table and joined the other three in a seat. A servant walked in and brought each of the two newcomers a cup of hot chocolate also.

"Your majesty!" A different servant ran into the room, obviously in a state of panic. "Sombre has sent word that he is prepared for battle and is ready to fend off any attack we throw at him. What shall we do?"

There was a moment of stunned silence. Then Luci spoke. "I knew from the beginning that this was what it was going to come to, but after actually being there with Sombre... he could have killed me when he caught me in his library, but he didn't. He... was actually kind to me. He trained me." She looked at Alric. "My powers... they're even stronger now. He helped me to control the shadow side of them."

Alric's eyes went wide. "The shadow side?" he said in disbelief. "Luci, elves don't..."

But Luci was continuing, and Alric fell silent, a look of contemplation on his face.

"Please," Luci said, shaking her head. "Can't we... I don't know... make some sort of truce?"

Kirem spoke up. "Sombre may have shown you mercy, Luci, but he didn't do the same to the hundreds of people he burned in the fire." He gestured to Alric.

Alric looked up, suddenly very focused. "Luci," he said. "I know you have seen good in Sombre. But every person has some good. Perhaps he… saw something in you that touched him. Whatever the case," he continued, "he has mercilessly slaughtered hundreds of innocents, and continues his executions even now. He is a broken man, Luci, incapable of seeing wrong from right. He cannot be trusted, and he must be destroyed. No," he said. "He must pay for his crimes. Whether it's through battle, or through execution, he must die."

Luci was caught in a brief moment of conflict. She didn't want to kill Sombre as before, she couldn't betray him like that – especially not after he had trained her and opened her eyes to her true potential. She hadn't even had a chance yet to show the rest of them how strong she had become. Luci looked up, meeting Alric's eyes. "I know Sombre deserves to die," she said. "And his crimes are inexcusable. I know he can't be left to reign, and you're right that he can't be trusted; not with a kingdom, at least. But as just a man…"

Alric placed his hand on Luci's shoulder. "You have your mother's mercy in you, Luci. She had a heart for seeing the goodness in others. But one bit of good doesn't cover up all the bad."

"Can't we think of something?" Luci said. "What if I can get him to agree to step down?" She looked around at the others, meeting each of their eyes.

"I will not send you back in there to attempt a truce, Luci," Alric said. "It's too dangerous."

"His forces are preparing an attack as we speak, Luci," Kirem answered. "We must fight first to defend our people. Perhaps, if we are able to capture Sombre, you could speak with him. But he cannot be allowed to continue his reign of destruction. Leaving him free puts both of our kingdoms at risk. Whatever happens, he must be stopped."

Violet stepped forward toward Luci. She could see the glimpse of fear in Luci's face, a fear she recognized: the fear of losing someone she cared for. She put her arm around Luci, turning to face the others. "I trust Luci," she said. "If she sees good in him, it's there. But I agree he can't be trusted just running free. What if we can capture him and then make a compromise… What if we exile him from Beyaluna and Whitesmoke?"

"Yes," Luci agreed, hope on her face. "Let him live alone and away from any person. Spare his life, but let him suffer alone." Luci hated this compromise, but what more could she say? She swallowed and waited for Alric to say something.

Alric looked closely at Luci's face. "I'm sorry, Luci, but no. Too much is at stake. The kingdom. My people. You. This is my battle to fight, Luci. I left these people at Sombre's mercy, and now I must finish it. I must free them. Sombre cannot be allowed to live."

Kirem nodded slightly in agreement, though Luci could see sympathy in his eyes.

Luci bit her lip and nodded. "I understand," she said. Hot tears fought their way forward, and she blinked them back.

Violet squeezed Luci's shoulder and gave her a sad smile. "I'm sorry," she whispered.

"Your highness," a servant interrupted, poking in his head. "Sombre's forces are on the move. They will be here before sunset tomorrow."

Kirem stood there, speechless. Luci gasped and Alric growled. Alric told Luci they needed to select a weapon for her, and they quickly slipped out. Kirem suddenly rushed off toward his quarters, muttering about unknown things. The servant ran back out the door, following Kirem.

Violet stood entirely still. For a reason that was unknown to her, tears filled Violet's eyes. She quickly blinked them away, hoping that no one saw. She ran after Kirem calling out to him.

He ignored her and walked into his room and closed the door behind him, shutting out the servant and Violet. The servant shrugged and walked away. Violet turned around and ran after Alric and Luci. The two were shooting crossbows when Violet walked in. They immediately switched over to swords. Violet called out to them, but they were too focused to notice her. Violet growled and walked back inside. *How is it that everyone forgets about me? I mean, I know I'm no lost princess or anything, but still…* She trudged into her room and flopped on the bed, hoping that not one person walked into the door. But of course, someone opened her door. *Wow, just my luck.* Violet thought. She ignored whoever had entered. *It was probably just a servant, anyway.* She covered her face with her pillow. Someone tapped her shoulder and Violet peeked out from behind the pillow. Standing next to her bed was Kirem, looking incredibly worried. "We must leave to strike at Sombre in the morning. If we wait much longer, he will strike us first. You will stay here and keep watch over Whitesmoke."

"I want to go," Violet told him without a shred of doubt in her voice.

"No, you cannot," Kirem commanded Violet.

"Yes, I can!" Violet demanded. "I'm not a helpless child! I'm nineteen years old, and I can handle myself!"

Kirem looked worried, but finally caved in. He simply nodded.

Violet was now going into battle, and she was

somewhat glad. Kirem took her hand and they walked together to the armory. Kirem allowed her to pick out her armor and weapons. She went with a golden armor, a crossbow with a quiver of arrows, and a shiny sword. Now that Violet felt geared up, Kirem allowed her to wander. She managed to find her way to a balcony. Once she stood on it, Violet recognized it as the balcony that she saw when she first arrived in the kingdom. It was morning now. Their preparations had taken most of the night. She was exhausted, but the beautiful sunrise caused the white buildings that glowed in the sun to shine even brighter than ever before. The wind blew softly, making the trees sway slowly. Peace was everywhere, and nothing dared to disturb it. Violet sighed heavily. *The calm before the storm,* Violet thought. It was hard to worry when everything was like this, but Violet still managed to. She thought about losing everything she loved. She thought about losing Luci and Alric. What would life be like without her friends? Then she thought about Kirem. Violet made her way to the edge of the balcony, barely leaning over its railing. If Violet lost Kirem, she would never hear his laugh, she would never again see his soft eyes, feel his protection, touch his soft hands, or feel the warmth of his embrace. There would be no more comfort when she was sad, no more help when she needed it. Her heart sank into an ocean of sorrow, realizing that Kirem could be seriously harmed or worse in this battle. Even though Violet had only just met him, she felt an instant connection with him. It was strange to feel so much for someone she had known for such a short time. A single tear slid down Violet's cheek. Before it fell off her face, Violet felt a hand on her shoulder. She wiped the tear and spun around. Kirem stood there, smiling. He pulled Violet into an embrace, causing her to shed another tear. Kirem pulled back a little.

"What is wrong?" he asked.

"Just…" Violet paused, "Scared, I guess."

"I asked you not to come with us and you refused. You told me you were not a child. If you want to stay, I will gladly let you. You do not have to fight with us, Violet," Kirem said, trying to comfort her.

"It's not that," Violet said, holding back her tears.

"Than what, then? What is frightening you so?" Kirem asked. Worry was prominent on his face.

"The thought of losing my friends," Violet answered back. "Of losing you."

Kirem smiled, but only for a moment. "I am afraid of losing you, too Violet," he admitted.

The two stared at each other for a long time. Kirem slowly pulled Violet closer to him, and she didn't resist. Soon, they were so close that their noses brushed against each other. His warm breath fanned across her cheeks. This time was so very different than any other time they had been close. This time neither of them blushed because neither was nervous or embarrassed. This time they had each other. Violet felt Kirem's hand brush against her hair as he pulled her to him the rest of the way. His lips brushed against hers and she let her eyes flutter closed. She marvelled at how soft his lips were and how nice he smelled up close. Like pinewood and sunlight. He pulled away slightly but still held her to him, like if he let her go she might never come back.

"We should go inside and get some rest. Tomorrow will be difficult and we will need all of our strength," Kirem told her. Violet nodded her head in agreement and the two walked into the castle hand in hand, ready to face whatever was thrown at them.

Now the sun was fully risen and Kirem was rallying the Elves, preparing them for the upcoming battle. He gave them each armor and weapons. Once Violet was dressed in a suit of armor with her weapons in hand, the army began their trek to Beyaluna.

"So, you and my cousin, huh?" Luci said, sneaking up behind Violet. She was catching on to her new-found Elven abilities rather quickly.

"Shut up, Canada." Violet told her and Luci laughed. One last small moment of peace before their lives would change forever.

Chapter 11

Sombre's shadow warriors were fighting against the attacking rebels. The sounds of clashing metal swords rang through the air. Bow strings were being loosed, sending arrows flying all around them.

"Find who you believe needs the most help and fight with them," Kirem screamed over the noise. Everyone but Violet nodded.

"I'm staying with you," she told Kirem with a steely determination.

"Okay," he replied to Violet with softened eyes, "you can stay with me. Everyone else, let us go find people who could use our help."

The entire group separated. Violet and Kirem ran off in one direction while Alric ran the opposite way.

Luci looked around and felt immediately overwhelmed. Sweat was beading down her back, under her shirt, and along her forehead. Her breathing was shallow but she knew she couldn't chicken out now. She was a part of getting these people into this mess and she was going to help them out of it.

She pulled out her sword and began slashing at every shadow warrior that came within arm's reach of her or any of the people around her. So much anger, confusion, and frustration that had been building up inside of Luci was being released. Ever since she was tossed into Beyaluna, she had felt helpless, but now she was finally doing something about it.

War raged on all around Luci. She may not have known all of these people personally, but they were all fighting and dying for her father's cause, and even though she was doing all she could to help them, it still wasn't enough. Someone next to her fell to the ground and she jerked away from them, snapping out of her daze. It was a young man, not wearing any armor and not armed. Now he lay on the ground with his eyes open and unfocused. His chest wasn't moving.

All of a sudden Luci felt like she was about to be sick.

Luci looked around her again, taking in the loss and destruction that both sides were suffering. People were falling all around her and the screams were deafening. Some were from children who had just seen their parents die and others were from people who had just been directly harmed by one of Sombre's little monsters. Luci couldn't believe that all of this was happening because of the man who had shown her great mercy.

She made her way through the crowds of people as if she were just dreaming, her feet moving without direction but her eyes seeking out her friends, needing to know that they weren't the source of any of the screams. Her gaze landed on Violet and Kirem fighting side by side, moving together as if they were one being. Something behind them caught her eye. Her eyes drifted to the all-too-familiar figure in the background. Caven had his bow raised in the air, arrow ready to fly. Luci searched for where Caven was aiming, and when she saw it, all of the air got sucked from her lungs.

Luci's feet couldn't move her fast enough across the battle field. She couldn't focus on her glamour anymore, but she was so focused on her target that she didn't even notice when it slipped. Her focus was on the fact that she was not going to make it in time. She could feel her feet hitting the ground and the shin-splitting pain that shot up her legs, but she still couldn't move fast enough. She wasn't going to make it.

Caven let his arrow fly and Luci screamed. Violet and Kirem looked her way at the sound of her cry and they both immediately joined in. "Alric!"

Alric lifted his head and looked at Luci. His gazed locked into hers with a mix of love and concern. He didn't even see Caven.

She would never make it in time. Everything within her twisted in panic. "Alric!" she screamed again.

Everything froze around Luci. People stopped in the middle of motion, the breeze stopped in the middle of blowing, flags in the middle of flying. Alric was still staring at Luci, frozen in time. The arrow had just entered his chest, but the shock of pain had not yet spread to his face. Violet looked like a statue, as she was frozen right in the middle of chasing after Alric; Kirem was right behind her, frozen while reaching out his arm to grab hers.

There was movement in the corner of her eye and when Luci looked in that direction, she saw Caven running up the castle steps and through the doors. Without giving it a second thought, she chased him into the castle, not thinking about Alric because she knew she was already too late. All she could do now was seek vengeance for her father and punish the person who took him from her before they even got the chance to know each other.

Violet heard Luci scream and she spun around to see what was wrong. She followed Luci's gaze and understood why she was screaming. Violet started running toward Alric before she even thought to do it. She was almost there; she could practically feel Alric under her palm. Violet felt Kirem's hand on her arm right before everything went still. Everything around her stopped moving all at once, even the arrow that was heading straight for Alric's chest, and she couldn't even bring herself to move. Almost immediately after, she saw Luci chase somebody into the castle and Sombre follow closely behind.

Sombre was directing his soldiers, sending them to flank left and right around small groups of the rebels, cutting them off from one another. The battle was almost like an intricate dance to him, and his forces responded effortlessly to his wordless commands. Out of the corner of his eye, he noticed one soldier in black garb moving against his orders. He recognized the man; he was a servant who worked often in the banquet halls. But why was he on the battlefield? Sombre watched as the servant nocked and arrow and took aim. He followed the servant's gaze and took in a sharp breath. Alric. He truly was there. If this servant was successful, the battle could all be over in an instant. Sombre would reward this man handsomely for his actions in service to his king. Sombre held his breath and watched. In the instant the arrow released, Sombre felt a small surge – a flicker – to his left. He turned. It was Luci, his apprentice. She should have been inside the castle, not out here in the fray. And why was she in the garb of the rebellion? Luci's body stiffened. She had seen the servant loose his arrow and was running. Was it possible – she seemed to be trying to *save* Alric. She was running toward him with lightning speed. Speed not unlike – there it was again, the flicker. Luci's hair flashed from dark to orange and back again. Her body seemed to get taller, then shrink again. *Could it be?* Sombre watched intently as Luci flickered again, and he felt the small surge of power as the glamour fell away. Her features snapped into place, her body lengthened, and bright orange curls sprang out from where straight, dark hair had been before. Her eyes were a glowing purple. Sombre's heart skipped a beat. And still, the girl ran. She screamed out one single word: *Alric!* Suddenly everything went still. The whole battlefield was frozen in time. But the girl was not, and neither was the servant. Sombre watched as Luci sped after the fleeing archer, and followed quickly behind them, his mind racing. *The girl was an elf. How could he have missed it? And calling out for Alric like that… certainly the girl wasn't -- or could she be?*

Chapter 12

The battle raged on in front of Sombre's castle. Large catapults were launching balls of fire from the wall of the castle towards the rebels in attempt to cause them to retreat. Sombre's forces were fighting hard, but the rebels were fighting back harder. Houses were burning to the ground. Almost everything was on fire, except the castle. A few Elves and rebels attempted to save some of the citizens from the fire, but they couldn't save everyone. Buildings crashed to the ground, crushing anything and anyone in their path. No matter how many were killed, the shadows kept on coming. When one was struck down, another one soon took its place. Not even the Elves could keep the shadows at bay. Sombre's army forced the rebels back, keeping them away from the castle and the Shadow King that locked himself inside, watching over them from a window. As the rebels continued to fight, a group of brave Elves tried to break into the castle, kill the king, and end the war. They made it to the draw bridge, only to realize the king had archers protecting the only entrance. The archers fired towards the rebel army, killing many. The draw bridge began to open, letting a strange figure out of the castle. He held a bow and arrow in his hands, ready to attack. Luci came running towards the bridge. She turned her head to see the figure. She then began to chase him, letting her glamour slip. Violet stood by Alric and Kirem when the figure fired the arrow at him. She screamed his name loudly, but it was too late.

This entire scene now stood frozen, as if preserved. Of the entire battlefield, the small figures of Caven, Luci, and Sombre were the only things in motion.

On the other side of the field, a misty blue disk hovered in the air. A person was partially through the portal, held in place by the stoppage of time.

Chapter 13

"You lied." Luci's voice dripped with anger.

Caven was still, his disgusting smile the only indication he was alive.

"You had no special power. You just wanted me to get caught for mine."

He smiled sweetly. "Anything else?" he said.

Luci seeped with rage. She raised her crossbow, pulled back on the string, and released. The arrow pierced the air, spiraling till it hit the stone wall. Caven turned and scurried down the hall, tunic flying behind him. Luci ran after him.

All her life had been a lie. The life she could have had – covered by deceit.

Up ahead, Caven turned right. The library. He pulled back the tapestry and entered the room with the spiral staircase. A little knot formed in Luci's upper belly, just under her heart.

Luci was ready to faint when she reached the top of the stairs. The door leading into the library was wide open. She, hot from the climb and with anger, slowly stepped into the soft moonlight reflecting from the marble, and slammed the door behind her. She grew paler, her eyes darker. Her appearance was something of a shadow.

"Caven!" she growled. "I know you're here!" Luci strode up and down the rows of books like a predator. Her breathing was tense, constricted. The hairs on the back of her neck prickled with sweat. She peered through the bookshelves. *Thud.* Caven had pounced from the top of the bookshelf behind her. *How did he get up there? No time.* He ducked backwards before Luci's arrow could pierce him. Now on the floor, he scooted backwards on all four limbs like a crab, his shadow bobbing in sync.

In a second he sprung up, surprising Luci. "I should tell you – you were wrong earlier."

Luci had her sword out now, slashing back and forth, Caven staying only inches away and not running altogether. He was toying with her, and this only fueled Luci's rage. She slashed harder, drawing him closer and closer to the oval windows.

Caven continued. "You were wrong, Luci. Are you surprised?" The whites of his eyes turned the same color as his blue iris, piercing Luci's with such intensity that she had to look away. Luci faltered in her sword slashing. *What was he talking about?*

In a flurry, Luci was pushed up and crashed down on the marble floor. Her head banged and the air was sucked out of her lungs.

She was held there as Caven drew closer, spite and sick pleasure in his completely blue eyes. "You are so completely blind, Luci. Did you not stop once and think, 'Why does he need that book?'"

Luci squirmed under his hold. Her sword fell from her hands. Power surged through her veins, but Caven pinned her down still.

"I was captured in the neighboring forests of Beyaluna," Caven said. "I lived with my people in peace. Until Sombre's shadow warriors took me as a slave. Through my visions, I have seen the truth about you. A punch to you is a punch to Sombre."

Luci faced the windows; the moon's light almost blinded her. Caven's silhouette advanced, but Luci gained some independence and stood.

"What do you mean?" she said. Her voice echoed.

He said nothing, coming at her with intensity. His hands were almost around her neck when something happened. A dark mist filled the air, swirling around Caven and Luci. Her eyes turned a blank white as she broke the spell Caven had on her. She began floating in the air, and her hair stood on end. The mist soon drew close to her, sinking into her heart. A black smoke seeped from her eyes as she began to transform. Her outfit soon changed to a long black dress that had no end, it only faded into mist at her feet. Her glowing white eyes soon went away, giving her normal eyes back. But something was different about her. She wasn't Elven, nor was she Luci. She was a dark and evil shadow. She held out her hand, and a mist shot out in the shape of a sword. It turned solid into a black sword radiating a weird red magic. Caven stood there, terrified.

"Who are you?" he asked, petrified.

Luci only laughed. She came back down on the ground and held her sword out at him. He pulled out his own sword, ready to duel. Their swords clashed in an epic battle raging on in the library. Luci swung her legs under Caven, tripping him. He was breathing heavily, and Luci was standing there without a scratch.

"Please don't harm me!" Caven begged. Luci looked into his eyes, and suddenly pictured him loosing the arrow at Alric, then running off like a coward. Rage seethed within her, and in that moment, Caven sensed her distraction and leapt. Luci reached out to protect herself, and a shadowy surge burst out from her against her control, making the room quake and sending Caven tumbling backward. His body made contact with the oval windows and shattered them. He fell through and hit the ground beneath. His bones cracked with the force.

The surge of shadow dissipated and shattered glass rained down everywhere, snapping Luci out of her trance. She gasped, realizing what she had just done. Her shadow form disappeared.

Behind her was the crunch of glass breaking under the weight of someone.

"Very good," a voice said. "Perhaps you are stronger than I thought."

Luci recognized the voice almost immediately. Sombre had been watching the whole time.

Chapter 14

Sombre stared at Luci. She frowned at him. He walked toward her, but she used her powers to hold him still. "How dare you?" she asked him.

"How dare I what?" Sombre asked her as if he had no clue what she was talking about.

"How dare you applaud me for that? I just killed that man!" Luci screamed at him. She had just thrown Caven out a window and he had the nerve to congratulate her?

"I could not help it. That was a spectacular display and an excellent use of your powers," Sombre said to her without emotion.

Through the broken window, Luci caught a glimpse of the battlefield. People were frozen in the middle of killing, of dying. "Sombre," Luci said, "you can't honestly think that this is the best thing for your people; that you're the best thing for these people. You just said that me killing someone was spectacular. These innocent people are out there dying and killing other living beings because they think it is the only way to survive."

It was as if Sombre's eyes were made of glass and Luci had just made a crack.

"Everyone else is out there fighting against you," she continued. "You've oppressed them so much that they're more willing to die than to live like that any longer." Luci could almost hear the new crack that she just made.

The cracked king stared at the ground in silence for a long time. Luci waited. Eventually he looked up.

"You look a lot like her, you know," he said. "My wife, I mean. She was… she and your mother were sisters. When I look at you, I can see glimpses of her."

Luci didn't know how to respond. She stood silently and waited for him to continue.

"I was not always like this," he said. "I was happy and I used my powers for good. I was about to have a family, you know." Sombre looked at Luci with eyes on the brink of tears. "I lost my wife and daughter and along with it, my control. I did not know what to do with myself and I lost my head…" His voice trailed off as he wandered over to a window, looking out over the frozen battlefield. "I felt so out of control," he said. "I knew my anger was harming people, but revenge was all I could think about. For 19 years… nothing but revenge." He looked up at Luci, meeting her eyes. "I did not realize how bad things got until it was too late. It is too late for me now, Luci."

"The people will never forgive you for what you've done and I'm not going to argue with you about that because it would be pointless, but that doesn't mean it's too late." Luci told him.

"What are you talking about?" Sombre asked.

"They won't forgive you and you definitely shouldn't be king, but you don't have to give up all hope. Just because you won't be in charge does not mean this kingdom doesn't have a future. You have good in you, too, Sombre." Luci said. "I've seen it. Make a truce with me. The rebels trust me, and I'll act as a representative for them. We'll go tell them that we've come to an agreement and that they need to stop their fighting. I can't guarantee that they'll be on board right away, but if you tell them exactly what you told me and that you're voluntarily giving up your position as king that you forcefully took to begin with, we might stand a chance of actually having peace again."

Sombre looked at Luci with wonder in his eyes at how such a young girl could be so wise.

"Who is going to rule the kingdom?" Sombre asked her. "After all I have done, I would understand if you did not think I care about this kingdom but I do. You are Alric's daughter, are you not?"

Luci looked at him in surprise.

"I am sorry," he said.

Luci knew what he meant, but she pushed the thought away. Her throat tightened and she felt hot tears rising to the surface.

"You are the rightful ruler, Lucilla;" Sombre continued. "You would make an excellent leader."

"I barely know these people; there's no way I can lead them. I'm going to propose a democracy."

The confused look on Sombre's face told her that she should explain further. "The people get to vote and choose who *they* want to lead them."

"I have never heard of a *democracy*, but I like it," Sombre said. "It will make the people very happy to have a say in who will be leading them." He gave a wistful smile.

"I thought it might be a welcome change," Luci said with a matching smile. "For now, we need to go out there and tell the people that you surrender to the rebels and that you will call off your troops."

"Okay," Sombre said, nodding his head. "I trust you, Luci."

The two walked out of the library and through the castle, passing the frozen people in the halls. Getting to the door, the pair opened it up and saw everyone frozen in the middle of fighting. *Alric.* Luci thought.

Luci dragged Sombre toward where Alric was, but before they could get there she passed a familiar blue and purple disk. Atara standing there frozen with one leg still on the other side of it. "Mom," Luci whispered, reaching out to touch her mother's shoulder.

As soon as Luci's hand made contact with her mother's shoulder, Atara unfroze and stumbled the rest of the way out of the portal. She blinked quickly, and her eyes locked onto Luci's. "Luci? Lucilla, it's you!" Atara took her daughter by her shoulders and pulled her into her chest for a hug. "When the school called and said you never showed up for classes, I was so worried; but when I came to your dorm and you were nowhere to be found, I just knew… I should have been here so much sooner, but I never was the strongest at portals and I haven't used my powers in 19 years… Luci, I'm so sorry. This must have been so terrifying for you." Suddenly she noticed what was going on around them. Her eyes went wide and she pulled back, holding Luci at arm's distance. "I haven't seen anything like this since… Luci, are you okay?" She examined Luci all over, checking her face, her hands. "Are you hurt?" she asked.

"Mom!" Luci pulled Tara into a hug again, and Tara relaxed, hugging back. Luci breathed in the smell of her mother, so familiar and yet almost nostalgic, like something from a distant past. She wrapped her arms around her mother and held her tight, feeling her warmth.

Suddenly, Atara pulled back. "What are you doing with him?" she asked in disgust, looking over Luci's shoulder at Sombre.

"There's a lot I need to tell you, Mom," Luci told her in a soothing tone. "But right now we need to stop this battle. Sombre has agreed to a truce. He's going to call off his troops and hand the kingdom back over to the people."

"Luci, I don't know what you've been told since you've been here, but I'm confident in saying that you aren't fully aware of what's happening here," Atara told her.

"What do you mean? I know that Sombre has been awful and that he burned the kingdom but he told me why. He was grieving and even though that's no excuse for what he did, I think I might be able to get the people to accept his offer of a truce," Luci explained.

"That's not what I meant, Luci," Atara told her.

"I know, Mom," Luci said. "Alric told me the rest. He said that he and Aeryn are my parents. You were Aeryn's lady's maid and friend."

"Luci, no," Atara responded. "That isn't exactly –"

"Why would they lie to me about that?" Luci interrupted.

"He didn't know he was lying to you, Luci. We need to sit down for us to talk about this before you do anything else." She looked up at Sombre. "You need to hear this too, Sombre," she said.

"Mom, what's going on?" Luci asked. The three of them walked over to the grass to sit in the shade of a tree.

"Aeryn had a twin sister named Ariana," Atara began.

Luci could audibly hear Sombre's breath hitch at the sound of this.

"I was Aeryn's lady's maid and another woman was Ariana's," Atara continued. "Ariana married Sombre and Aeryn married Alric. Everything happened at the same time. Both girls were courted and married at the same time. They were even pregnant at the same time."

Luci felt the wind knocked out of her. *I have a cousin? Sombre has a child? I thought he said he lost his wife and child.*

"They gave birth on the same day to two beautiful baby girls. Ariana died in childbirth, and so did Aeryn's baby." Atara had tears running down her face as she spoke. *What is she talking about? Aeryn's baby didn't die.*

"But mom, I'm sitting right here. I'm alive." Luci told her mother, confused.

"I know you are, princess," Atara told her with a hand on her shoulder, "but you aren't Aeryn's daughter. Your mother was Aeryn's sister."

Sombre stopped breathing for a minute.

Luci did too. *Alric wasn't my father, Sombre was. My father was the one who hurt all of these people.*

"That is impossible," Sombre said, breathless. "Alric poisoned both my wife and child. He killed them, so I burned his kingdom to the ground and took his people from him. It is what he deserved."

"Alric's child died," Atara explained. "He didn't poison your family, Sombre. Your wife died in childbirth but your daughter is very much alive. When Ariana realized she had been poisoned, she called for me and begged me to take the child to Aeryn. She feared the baby would be a target as well. The baby's safety was her dying plea. Aeryn took the baby as her own at her sister's request and we both swore never to tell anyone. The body of Aeryn's baby was given a funeral alongside Ariana, and weeks passed. Then the fire came and we fled the city. Aeryn opened the portal to make sure we could get away, but then she returned to the castle for Alric and when she didn't come back, I took Lucilla through the portal myself because I promised my best friend that I would keep her safe." Atara was now fully crying from reliving the memory of her best friend's death. She sniffled and wiped the tears from her eyes. "Sombre, I am so sorry for keeping Luci from you. I was afraid. Aeryn trusted me to take care of her, and the last I knew of you was that you had burned Beyaluna and killed everyone in it. I couldn't bring myself to give her to you. I was afraid I would be disappointing Aeryn."

"I understand, Atara. I would not have known what to do with a child. I was too caught up in my rage and grief," Sombre told her. His eyes were understanding but his face still showed signs of him being in shock. "I am glad Luci thought Alric was her father, even though it was false. I would not have wanted her thinking that her true father was purely evil."

Alric! Luci had forgotten until now. *Everything was still frozen; was it possible she could save him?* She scrambled up off of the ground as quickly as possible and ran to Alric, her heart racing. Halfway there she noticed someone move. They lowered their raised sword with a confused look on their face. *No.* Luci looked around and saw that everyone was now moving. *No!*

She was too late. By the time Luci reached Alric, Violet was already sobbing
violently over him and Kirem was crying silently while cradling Violet in his arms.

Chapter 15

The rebels looked around for possible survivors. Luci watched them as they looked through the rubble of what used to be their houses. Only a woman and her child were found so far. The woman had red hair and fair skin. Her son had fiery orange hair. The clothes were torn and they were covered in bruises and cuts. The boy only suffered from a minor concussion, while his mother had a broken arm. Luci saw them sitting there, terrified any time they heard a pebble hit the ground. Behind Luci, there was a house still standing. The windows were gone, however. Luci turned away from the house. She looked at the ground to see shattered glass all around her. She gasped and backed up, tripping over a stump and falling to the ground. She quickly stood up and ran into the castle. She got all the way into the throne room and sat on a large seat next to the throne. In the far corner of the room, Luci saw Violet sobbing into Kirem's arms. Luci stood up and tiptoed slowly out of the room, not wishing to disturb them. Once she made it out of the room, Luci bumped into Sombre. He stood there, a little bit happy for an unknown reason.

"Luci," Sombre said, "do you wish to continue reading in the library?"

Luci thought about the library, and heard glass shattering again.

"No!" Luci said, "I mean, no thank you. I just need some privacy."

"Ah, I see," Sombre replied, "Do you miss Alric already? Your friend in there does."

"Yes," Luci confessed, "But not as much as her. Violet was attached to him. Or at least, that's what Kirem said." Sombre nodded. A loud sob was heard, but it soon slowly disappeared.

"Usually, I would be delighted to see someone upset," Sombre began, "Being a shadow, I feed off of fear, anger, and dismay. Hence why I was a truly awful king. Without those emotions being constantly here, I would surely cease to exist."

"So, you would die?" Luci summed up.

"Not precisely," Sombre said, "It's more like we fade away from existence and we are removed from everyone's memory." Luci looked at him, a little bit frightened.

"Aren't you just a little ray of sunshine?" Luci sarcastically said.

"I'm not," Sombre replied, confused. "I am an evil shadow. Or, I used to be evil." Luci laughed at Sombre's misunderstanding of the term. She began to explain, until Sombre interrupted her.

"I wasn't exactly the greatest king," Sombre said out of nowhere, "and I think I should give my throne to the heir."

Luci gave him an *Are you being serious?* look. "I already told you, I'm no queen," she said. "These people need a ruler who knows how to lead them. They need someone they trust. They have the right to choose."

Sombre smiled and took off his crown and handed it to her. It quickly changed into a flower crown when Luci touched it. The flowers were made of multiple sparkling gems, all glowing with a dazzling mist around them. Some flowers were a vibrant neon, while others were pastel, and some were a plain black gem. The vines that intertwined with each other were made out of gold, shining almost as bright as the flower gems. On one part of the crown, there was a pink butterfly sitting on a black flower. It was the most beautiful thing Luci had ever seen. Luci handed the crown back to Sombre and it immediately changed back into the spiked black form it was before.

"I'll think about it." Luci smiled at Sombre and put a hand on the crown. Half of it turned back into the flower crown almost instantly. "Thanks…dad."

As her hand left the crown, the flower crown disappeared again. Sombre nodded, bowed slightly, and left the room, leaving Luci to herself. She turned around to see

Violet leaving the throne room behind her. Violet waved slightly at Luci, and Luci waved back.

"Glad to see you're feeling better," Luci told her friend.

"Just because I'm not crying, doesn't mean I feel any better," Violet snapped back.

Luci nodded in reply. She watched as Violet trudged out the door to Luci's right. She walked out and towards the drawbridge, with Luci right behind her.

The hurt and broken rebels waved and cheered as Luci walked behind Violet and out to the rubble. This made Luci feel guiltier than anytime she had ever done something wrong. *What is wrong with me?!* Luci thought. *How many things can a girl do wrong in a day?! Let's see. I killed Caven, I let Alric die, I caused all these rebels to die, I can't cheer up Violet, and I disobeyed my mo – I mean, caretaker, which got me here in the first place!* Luci felt like she had failed Beyaluna and everyone in and out of it. The once-burnt land was now scorched because of her. Or at least, she thought so.

Violet, on the other hand, was sure it was all Sombre's fault. He was nothing but a tyrant and an evil shadow who had plagued the land for far too long. Violet grumbled as she walked through the rubble, soon losing Luci to a crowd of rebels begging to see her. Violet saw a small child run up to her, smiling and laughing.

"Lady!" he called out, "I found my mommy!" Violet now smiled with him, recognizing him almost instantly.

"I told you we would find her," Violet replied. He hugged her legs and ran back to a woman. She looked almost exactly like her son. The only difference was their eye color. The boy had bright blue eyes and his mom had black eyes. They both had pale brown hair and pale skin with no blemishes to be found. Violet's smile soon faded, and she thought of her own mother. *What would she think if I left her and lived here?* Violet thought. She soon got rid of the thought. It made her think of her dad, both her biological dad and Alric, far too much. She saw Kirem close to the castle. Violet made her way back over and saw him talking to Luci.

Luci and Kirem were talking about how they could help with the damage. Luci turned her head to see Violet coming back with a slight smile. Kirem soon put his protective arm around her, making her smile a little wider.

"So..." Violet said, "Are we staying or leaving?"

Luci shrugged, obviously just as indecisive as Violet.

"Whatever we choose, it will be the right choice," Luci replied, "I hope."

Violet pushed the decision from her head. It was far too hard to think about now. They all fell silent, and soon walked back into the castle for a good night's rest.

Chapter 16

"Luci, don't be afraid."

Luci followed behind Kirem, who guided her up the steps to the executioner's stage. The last time she was here was during that woman's execution, then there were the shadow warriors chasing her and Violet, then the start of her involvement with the rebellion. A dizzying, overwhelming feeling was being brought upon her, and she thought she was going to be sick. She stalled.

The entire city of Beyaluna was called to be here. They gathered around in a circle, like they had always done at executions, and that was what they were expecting. Luci felt small in their presence. She was relieved when Kirem told her that Violet and he would stand behind her, to show their support for her as their leader.

Kirem cleared his throat. His voice echoed in the square. "People of Beyaluna, I am Kirem, son of Whitesmoke, son of Dryden. I speak to you with a heavy heart, for we come with both great happenings –" he turned to Luci with a brief smile, then back to the crowd, now somber, "and sorrowful ones."

Luci's heart beat quickly in her ears. Kirem would call her up any second now.

"I leave these both to Luci Jones of Canada."

Luci walked to the center of the wooden stage, and was plagued by the thought that people had died there, for so many years, living under the Shadow King's reign. It had finally come to an end. This gave her courage. Luci went through the talking points in her head, and sincerely wished she had tried harder at Speech in school. She inhaled deeply and focused on projecting her voice.

"Um he-hello." Luci stuttered. Looking out at the crowd of people staring up at her, all Luci saw were hundreds of sets of blinking eyes, each one clouded with confusion. Before she knew it the words just began flowing out of her.

"Some of you know me. My name is Lucilla. My father was the true king of Beyaluna, Alric Howell."

Right then the entire crowd gasped. Eyes went wide and hands shot up to cover their mouths gone slack with shock.

"As many of you know already, it this same Alric who led the rebellion, and he was killed in the battle." Luci's voice began to crack. Even now knowing Alric was not her father, it still pained her to think about it. She closed her eyes and took a deep breath. "You believed for many years that you lost your princess in the same fire that you lost the rest of your royals. Actually, your princess was lost much sooner. Alric believed me to be his daughter and told me as much. I believed him and it wasn't until earlier that discovered he was mistaken. I was not his daughter but his niece."

Some people's eyebrows drew together in confusion and other faces contorted in comprehension of what she had said.

"Sombre is my father."

The crowd erupted in anger.

"Please calm down!" Luci shouted back at the crowd. "All I ask is that you hear me out," she stated calmly. "I have talked Sombre down and convinced him to give back the crown he had no right to to begin with. I propose a democracy. I know that many of you don't understand what I'm talking about, but all it means is that you get to choose who wants to rule you."

The people looked as if they were trying to process the new information they had been given.

"Just because I am the next in line for the throne doesn't mean I want it. I have no plans to take the throne forcefully. You have had that for too long already." Luci paused and thought hard, careful to choose her next words wisely, "In a couple of days, we can hold a free election. You will be able to cast your vote on whom you believe should next rule over Beyaluna." Luci looked down at her feet sheepishly before she turned herself around and quickly walked off of the executioner's stage.

Chapter 17

Luci paced back and forth in front of the throne in the castle. Thoughts of Canada and Beyaluna crossed through her head. Which should she stay in? Beyaluna had people needing her help, but Canada was where she was raised. They were both, in some way, her home.

"Luci," Atara said behind her, "The portal is ready to open."

Luci nodded.

Atara stopped Luci's pacing and touched her shoulder. "You don't have to go."

"I do!" Luci protested. "I think…"

Atara smiled at her. She walked out the door, leaving Luci to think.

"Hey there!" Violet called out almost immediately after Atara left. "Are you coming or going?"

Luci only shrugged.

Violet nodded. "I think I already know *my* answer…"

As if it was planned, Kirem came in right then.

"Hello, Luci," Kirem said, waving to her.

Violet rushed over and grabbed him by the arm, pulling him toward Luci. She squeezed them both into a group hug.

Kirem blushed and pushed the girls away.

"Careful! I still have to look nice," Kirem said after Violet messed up his hair for ruining the group hug.

Violet only laughed, and Kirem reached over and messed up Violet's hair.

"Oh, it's on!" Violet grabbed a pillow off of the throne and smacked Kirem with it.

He grinned, grabbed another pillow, and hit Violet with it.

Luci stood there laughing while Violet and Kirem continued their war.

The door opened, and Sombre came walking through. He raised his eyebrow at the whole event.

Violet stole Kirem's pillow, laughing maliciously. He gasped at the new double threat and ran down the hallway with Violet in hot pursuit.

"Have you decided yet, Luci?" Sombre asked his daughter.

"Um…" Luci thought for a little while. "Yes, I have."

"Good. Atara has sent me to fetch you."

"Tell her I choose –" Luci started, "Actually, I kind of want to tell her myself."

Luci hugged her father while Atara summoned the swirling blue disk that had brought them there in the first place.

Sombre kissed Luci's forehead.

"I still don't understand why you have to live so far away," Luci told him.

"I know," Sombre replied. "But it's what must be done."

Luci nodded and turned towards Violet. She was hugging Kirem tight.

"I hope we see each other soon," Violet told Kirem.

"We will," he assured her.

"Also, one more thing." Violet stood on her tippy toes and planted a kiss on Kirem's cheek. He blushed bright red. Violet only giggled and approached Luci.

Kirem and Sombre said their goodbyes, gave their parting hugs to everyone, and left.

Luci turned to Violet. "Are you sure you want to stay here with me?" Luci asked her best friend.

"Absolutely," Violet replied.

Atara finally brought forth the portal. The girls held each other's hands tight.

"Are you two ready to fulfill your destiny?" Atara asked them.

They nodded.

"Then I'll leave you to it," Atara said. "Luci," she said, placing her hand on Luci's cheek and looking into her eyes. "I am so proud of you."

She turned to Violet and grabbed her hand. "Thank you, Violet," she said. "Luci was very lucky to have a roommate like you."

"I always get the crazy ones," Violet answered with a crooked smile.

Luci hugged Atara tight. The portal opened itself.

Atara waved goodbye as she walked into the portal, leaving the girls behind in this world of wonder. Luci sighed as the portal closed in on itself. She would miss her mom, but she finally felt like she had found where she belonged.

Epilogue

The wind is blowing softly and the leaves on the trees are rustling. It sounds like the woods are whispering. The sun shines brightly down through the foliage, casting down a golden light on everything in sight. Luci takes in the beauty of her home as she walks the cobblestone path to the castle's greenhouse. The stones are warm from the sun under her bare feet.

Luci opens the glass door to enter the greenhouse and a small breeze causes the hairs falling from her up-do to brush lightly against the back of her neck. In the years following the rebellion, the greenhouse had been restored to its former glory. Looking all around her in every direction, Luci can see flowers of all different colors. She can faintly hear the sound of the fountain running in the middle of it all.

Walking through the winding paths towards the fountain, Luci takes a moment to stop and look at all of the flowers and admire the ones right about to bloom. Nearing the fountain, the sound of running water gets louder. Right there, right next to it, are three headstones and a small memorial.

Aeryn Rose Howell
1940-1960
Beloved queen, princess, wife, and sister

Alric Vitruvius Howell
1940-1979
Respected king and loving husband

Ariana Noel Orestes
1940-1960
Beloved princess, wife, and sister

Three headstones for three people very dear to this kingdom and very important to Luci. She gets down on the ground and runs her fingertips delicately over the small memorial stone.

Rhea Howell
1960
A beautiful princess who is much loved

A memorial for her cousin whom she never got to know. Luci sits down completely in front of the graves with her legs crossed and her purple dress splayed out on the ground around her. She comes out here as often as possible to talk to and be close to them. Even though they can't talk back and Luci knows that they're always with her, there's something special about being here that brings her a sense of peace. Over the years, Luci feels like she's gotten to know a lot about her real mother and who she was.

"Queen Lucilla, you need to leave for your meeting."

Luci turns around and sees one of her lady's maids standing a few feet behind.

"Okay, I'm coming; just give me a minute, please," Luci responds.

The woman nods her head and quickly turns around to exit the greenhouse.

Luci takes one final look at the graves. "I hope you guys are proud of what I'm doing with the kingdom," she whispers. "I'm doing my best to take care of them." She stands up, smoothing over her skirt and straightening the small crown resting on her head.

"Auntie Luci!"

Before she can react, two little bodies are running into her and hugging her legs. "Oof." She says, stepping back to gain her balance after the impact. "I just saw you two last week!"

"We're always excited to see you Auntie Luci," the little girl says.

"Yeah, Auntie Luci; when mommy and daddy told us you were coming we were so excited," the little boy says, nodding his head up and down as if that would convince Luci of his sincerity.

"Well, I'm always excited to see you guys, too."

The two children squeeze Luci's legs tighter and bury their faces in her dress.

"Eden, Cullen, at least let Aunt Luci get in the door first before you attack her."

Luci looks up to see a smiling Violet standing in the doorway.

"But mommy, we wanted to be the first ones to see her," the little girl Eden says.

"It's okay, Violet, I don't mind," Luci tells her, looking down at the kids. "Why don't we go out to the garden to have our tea?"

"Yeah!" the kids call at the same time.

"Go on, I'll meet you out there," Luci tells them with a smile on her face.

"Okay!" Cullen cries before grabbing his sister by the arm and dragging her out to the gardens.

"Good to see you again," Violet says, coming up to give Luci a hug.

"Good to see you, too, Vi," Luci says into the hug before pulling away. "You sure do have your hands full with those two, huh?"

"One five year old would be enough, but two?" Violet says with a sigh, as the two begin following the kids to the garden, but the smile sitting on her lips betrays her. "I should've known that twins would run in the family."

"They're beautiful kids." Luci opens the door out to the garden and lets Violet through first.

"And they adore their Aunt Luci. They look forward to every visit," Violet tells her with a smile.

"I adore them just the same," Luci says.

"Luci! So glad you made it okay." Kirem walks up to her in long strides and gives her a hug.

They stand there together, relishing the feeling of family. They are just about all each other have left. Kirem's parents died a couple of years ago and Luci has Sombre but he's living up in the mountains and she doesn't see him very often. Atara comes to visit them both on a regular basis but her permanent residence is still in Canada.

"Of course, Kirem."

They hold each other for what feels like forever. Luci counts his heartbeats and feels his chest rise and fall against her cheek with every breath. She reminds herself that he is alive and well and not going anywhere before she pulls herself away and they sit down together at the table.

"How is everything going in Whitesmoke?" Luci asks.

"Everything is going well," Violet says while Kirem pours the three of them tea.

"Everyone is happy. We are happier than we were even before the war. Back then there was a constant threat and now we are once again living in harmony," Kirem says wistfully, looking at his children playing in the flowers and blowing dandelions at each other. "We are free to let our children play in the gardens again without fear that something might happen to them."

Violet takes a hold of his hand and smiles at him comfortingly. "How are things in Beyaluna?"

"Everyone is happy as far as I know," Luci tells them. "I've never been in charge of a kingdom before and I'm still trying to get the hang of it. Something new comes up every day and I have to figure out how to handle it."

"You can always come to me for help, Luci," Kirem tells her. "I have only been running a kingdom about as long as you have, but I was raised being taught how, so I do have some knowledge."

"Look at us," Violet says in amazement. "It seems like just yesterday we were worrying about our first day of college and now here we are, eight years later, me married with two kids and both of us as queens of our own kingdoms."

"Yeah, where did the time go?" Luci looks over at the children playing in the flowers. Cullen got Kirem's silver hair and when the sun hits it, it's as if his hair was glowing. Eden's royal blue sundress contrasts her golden blonde hair beautifully. None of them know exactly where she got that hair from. However, both of them have the same purple eyes as Luci. Apparently it's a relatively common Elven trait. Other than that they look exactly alike, eerily so for being fraternal twins. They look so happy with wide smiles and loud giggles coming from their direction.

The two see Luci looking at them and wave her over.

"I will go and play with them," Kirem volunteers. "You two talk; it seems as if you both could use it." With a small smile at both of them, he leaves to go play with his children.

"I still can't believe you're a mother," Luci tells Violet. "When I met you, all you could think about was adventure and living your life to the fullest. Now you seem to be happily settled down."

"I did love adventure and I still do. Every day with my kids is an adventure all its own, and Kirem," Violet pauses to think for a moment. A blissful smile finds its way to her face before she says, "Kirem is my ultimate adventure. I feel like with him next to me, I could do anything."

"You guys are so amazing. You were meant to be together even if it meant that you had to cross into another dimension to do it," Luci tells her with a hand on Violet's shoulder.

With people all around her to help open a portal, Violet has been able to visit her mother on a regular basis. She's met Kirem and the kids but she thinks they live in Canada and she doesn't know what they do for a living, but Violet's mother isn't exactly nosy.

"You have been doing an amazing job, Luci. Nothing that has happened in the last eight years has been easy on anybody. I know you say you aren't ready to look for anyone special right now but one day you will be and you'll find the person you were always meant to be with," Violet tells her with genuine sincerity.

"Thank you, Vi," Luci says. She gives Violet a hug that is quickly returned.

"I better go relieve Kirem of watching those two," Violet says. She stands up out of her chair and walks over to the children and Kirem. Her yellow dress matches the sunlight. They look like the picture-perfect family.

Kirem walks over to Luci and sits at the table with her, watching Violet laugh as she tickles Eden and Cullen. "How have you been, Luci?" he asks her.

"I'm doing okay, actually," She says with a nod of her head as if to prove her point.

"And the nightmares?" he asks.

"I'm still having them but they aren't as bad now," Luci tells him.

"Have you been doing what I said? Telling yourself that everything is okay and writing down all of your dreams?" Kirem asks, his head cocked to the side and his arms resting on the table.

"Yes. I've been writing everything down, even the nightmares. And every time I wake up, I tell myself that everything is over, everyone is happy, and I'm safe," Luci explains. Ever since the battle she's been having terrible nightmares. She can still see the arrow in Alric's chest and hear the sound of the glass shattering when she sent Caven flying through the window.

"That is excellent, Luci. These feelings may never go away, but it will get easier to handle. You are doing an amazing job taking care of yourself and the people of Beyaluna. I am so glad my children have someone like you to look up to." Kirem takes her hand in his and looks Luci in the eyes.

"I'm thankful that I have them to keep me grounded. Without them watching me, I think I would've gone off the deep end a long time ago," Luci tells him. A single tear is now making its way down her cheek. Her gaze wanders over to see Violet lying in the grass with Eden and Cullen next to her, giggling and pointing to funny-shaped clouds in the sky.

"Their innocence shows us how unnecessarily complicated we make our lives," Kirem tells her. "They have changed all of our lives for the better." He stands up and holds out his hand, motioning for Luci to come with him.

They walk over to Violet and the kids. Eden and Cullen jump up to greet their father with enthusiastic squeals and hugs.

"Daddy! Come look at the clouds with us!" Eden says.

"I found a bunny!" Cullen claims proudly.

"And I found a pony!" Eden rivals.

"Excellent job, guys." Kirem ruffles Cullen's hair and kisses the top of Eden's head. They lie back down next to Violet, and Kirem kisses her forehead before lying down next to them.

Luci smiles at the scene in front of her. She never had any other family besides her mother and now she has these amazing people to call her family. People who will support and love her through anything. That's more than she ever could've asked for.

"Auntie Luci, will you look at the clouds with us?" Cullen asks, looking up at her with his wide purple eyes.

"Pretty please, auntie Luci?" Eden adds.

"Of course I will." Luci smiles at the two happy children. She lowers her back into the plush green grass and looks at the bright blue sky that's scattered with fluffy white clouds. *Everything bad is over*; the sky is clear and the sun is shining brightly down on their faces. *Everyone is happy*; Eden and Cullen are smiling and laughing at the little things in life. *I am safe*; Luci is surrounded by people who love her and make her happy.

Everything is well in the world for the new generation of royals in Beyaluna and Whitesmoke.

About the Authors

Lindy has been reading fantasy adventure stories late into the night since she was nine, and has wanted to write since before she could totally understand letters and words. It was the concept of communicating her original ideas and thoughts in detail that was (and still is) so appealing to her. She is in the process of writing a kids' fantasy series, and her biggest dream is to ruin the lives of her readers.

Emily Fertic is a 17-year-old high school student who was born and raised in Florida. She's been a lover of books for as long as she can remember; her need to put her own ideas on paper is what motivated her to start writing. *Beyaluna Burns* is one of her many projects and she strives to one day become a published author.

Gracie Sanchez is a middle school student in a high school class. She enjoys reading anytime, anywhere, any book. After a few years of non-stop reading, Gracie decided to write her own stories. Her mother took her and her brothers out of private school to homeschool. Three years into homeschooling, her mother discovered Class Source. She signed Gracie up for math, science, and eventually novel writing. To this day, Gracie is a homeschooler and loves to write and read for hours.

For more information

about the Class Source Collaborative Novel Writing program,
please visit our Facebook page at
https://www.facebook.com/ClassSourceNovel/
or email us at ClassSourceNovel@gmail.com.